# *THE TOR*

by

*Liza Granville*

BeWrite Books
www.bewrite.net

Published 1 internationally by BeWrite Books, Canada.
208 - 19897, 56th Avenue, Langley, BC, V3A 3Y1.

© Liza Granville 2010

The right of Liza Granville to be identified as the author has been asserted in accordance with sections 77 and 78 of the Copyright, Designs and Patents Act 1988. All rights reserved.

A CIP catalogue record for this book is available from the British Library

ISBN: 978-1-906609-22-1

Also available in eBook format.

Produced by BeWrite Books
www.bewrite.net

This book is sold subject to the condition that it shall not, by way of trade or otherwise, be lent, resold, hired out or otherwise circulated without the publisher's consent in any form other than this current form and without a similar condition being imposed upon a subsequent purchaser.

This book is a work of fiction. Any similarity between the characters and situations within its pages and places or persons, living or dead, is unintentional and co-incidental.

Artwork © Tony Szmuk 2010

'Reality is merely an illusion, albeit a very persistent one.'
*Albert Einstein*

For all those that blunder on,
keeping faith with Her,
come what may.

## *About the Author*

Liza Granville lives in Gloucestershire, UK, with three monstrous Persian cats and an over-active imagination. Her work is published in many magazines and anthologies. She has written three other novels: *Curing The Pig, The Crack of Doom* and *Until The Skies Fall.* Also a collection of short stories: *Baiting The Unicorn*

*THE TOR*

# 1

Jude's first small act of rebellion was swiftly followed by his first glimpse of the woman clothed in sky. She smiled. She beckoned. Her fine blue robe clung to every curve and he stood entranced, overcome by adoration, even while her eyes took possession of his soul and terror radiated from his gut, spreading right out to his fingers, his toes, into every strand of hair, every pore of his skin.

All morning they'd been travelling along an ancient greenway, worn deep and bordered by unfriendly, close-packed trees that turned it into a dark tunnel, sucking out every vestige of daylight. Soon the track began to climb. Fareed strained and panted, white froth laced his flanks, he wheezed and groaned. Everyone else – even Osker, hunched over today and coughing blood – dismounted and trudged wearily in the wagon's wake, but still Ma insisted that Jude stay perched on the box. He was precious. Anything might be lurking in the dense undergrowth.

The familiar arguments began. Ma silenced them, but not before Jude had overheard. They all thought he was a mammy-coddled grub, an idler, a spoiled brat. Jude didn't care. Why should he? Ma made sure he had the best of whatever food they came by, the warmest clothes, and the thickest blankets. But this time was different, an unexpected voice rose above the others, and when Osker spoke it was as well to listen, for it was a rare thing indeed now that his strength was failing so fast.

"You're doing the lad a disservice," he rasped. "It would be far better to harden him up. Let him learn some survival skills. If the worst came, how could he ever manage on his own? Besides ..." Osker coughed, a terrible choking sound, and a few seconds elapsed before he gasped out the rest. "Besides, Jude is almost a man. What have you done to prepare him for what must and will be faced?"

"Silence!" roared Ma.

"It is a task ..." began Osker.

Task? Jude leaned out of the wagon, hoping for more, but Ma was already yelling blue murder.

"*I* am the mother. The mother! Who are you to criticise how I raise my precious child? *THE* child. Task, indeed! Foolish stories! There is no task. *MAN*, indeed! Jude's hardly more than a baby."

"Fourteen summers by my reckoning," grumbled Bett. "Precious or not, here or there, now or then, plenty old enough to do what is needed."

"No," said Ma. "He is not. And there's an end to it."

"He bluddy is," said Tattow, and laughed knowingly.

"Jude must be prepared," insisted Osker. "It is long past time for telling him what must be done."

"That's right," said Bett. "You tell her. Perhaps she'll listen to you. I'm sick and tired of trying. I know what I know. There's change on the wind, the time's approaching fast, and if she don't do it soon, someone else will have to."

"Anyone who tries filling my child's head full of that sort of nonsense," bellowed Ma, "will be walking their own path. Let them see how they like that. No wagon. No group. No nothing."

"But it's your duty," ventured Bett.

"Hold your tongue, barren one."

"Soon," croaked Osker, raising his voice a little, "young Jude will make his own choices. He's been reared an idle youngster, but not a coward, we must all hope. When the sign comes, he'll do what must be done. Yes, he will, in spite of you."

A dull thwack followed. Jude's mouth fell open. It was a sound reminiscent of the playful slaps he sometimes aimed at Fareed's shoulder but, judging by the commotion that followed, playfulness had nothing to do with it. Something fell against the side of the wagon. There was a shout. And a sharp hiss. Summer started to wail. Ears back, the horse continued its patient shamble forward and Jude eased himself to the very edge of his seat so that he could peer round the canvas. Several paces behind now, Tattow and Bett were helping Osker to his feet. It seemed a painful process. Osker was bent almost double, folding his arms round his chest. He bit at the air while a thin line of blood trickled from the corner of his mouth. Ma strode behind the wagon, chin up and not looking at anybody.

Jude quickly slid back along the box. Fruits of the earth! She'd hit Osker! *Osker!* Ma was generous with her cuffs – however loudly she called him precious he'd learned early to duck away from sudden movements – but to strike poor sick Osker was surely going too far. As Jude sat automatically flicking aside overhanging branches, it occurred to him that he'd never questioned Ma's behaviour before. But then, apart from a few grumbles, none of them did.

The track's gradient increased sharply. The echoes of Fareed's labouring breaths ricocheted back from the deep banks. A faint glimmer of light appeared, far ahead. They were approaching the highway and in a few minutes one or other of the group would be sent forward to do The Road Thing. An idea occurred to him, and the more he thought about it, the more appealing it grew. Jude shuffled along the box again and saw that the others had fallen quite a way behind: Tattow and Summer were supporting Osker, Bett was shuffling through fallen leaves for nuts, and as for Ma, she was carefully stripping a clump of platter mushrooms from a rotten trunk.

A few yards ahead the track levelled out for a short stretch before climbing even more steeply towards the light. Here, Jude pulled on the ropes, bringing Fareed to a stop. The old horse deserved a rest before that final ascent. Moreover the stationary wagon would block Ma's view. Afterwards, let her bawl and flip as much as she pleased. He knew how to do this. And hadn't Osker said he was almost a man?

Flat on his stomach Jude crawled along the ditch. At the edge of the highway he rose and began the ritual. Look to the left. Look to the right. Look left again. And then right. Look above. Turn this ear towards the sky; then the other. Lastly, he hunkered down, pressing the side of his cheek against a patch of blistered tarmac, feeling for any vibrations – of the marching feet of those that moved in packs, or the grind of wheels from rust wrecks that might throw fire. The highway had nothing to tell him: the way was clear. Jude straightened, noticing for the first time that the clouds in the west didn't look right. They were darker and heavier than any amount of rain could make them, almost metallic, and too low, so low that they seemed to bite down into the land. He supposed a mighty storm was gathering its strength. Jude switched his gaze back to the highway itself and saw that the track opposite was so choked with brambles that it would be difficult too persuade Fareed along it. With any luck, that wasn't their route.

Jude turned his face eastward. And there was the woman.

She hovered before a stand of dark yews so that her red-gold hair, her white skin and the azure dress, painted with clouds, spangled with silver stars and crescent moons, stood out in sharp focus against the green. Jude's mouth dropped open. He could see her breasts through the fine cloth, pert-nippled, round as apples, nothing like the heavy dugs of Ma and Bett. When she smiled and extended her hand, one finger beckoning him forward, Jude was gripped with terror so profound that he was unable to move. The *down there* thing that he'd asked Tattow about also happened, and his face turned scarlet. He could hardly breathe. His body began to dissolve in a great golden purr that was abruptly obliterated by such terror that his vision turned black. It cleared for a split second to show him something that could not possibly be.

He was standing in an open square bounded by grim buildings so massively tall that only a pale sliver of sky forced apart their leaning tops. More people than he could ever have imagined pressed close on every side, elbowing and jostling forward, their faces set and determined, their mouths wide and angry as they brandished boards covered with rune marks. The sounds came a few seconds later – bawling and chanting, occasional screams, the clash of metal, the roaring of orders from men closing in on sleek, high horses. The crowd carried him forward. Missiles – rocks, stone slabs, iron bars – were hurled, scarcely a span above his head. Small fires erupted accompanied by whistling *cr-r-a-ck* sounds and deep hollow booms. A hand caught at his arm, but Jude fought it off and turned to run. Then a great mid-air stream of ice cold water struck him full in the chest, hard as an iron fist, knocking him to the ground and …

The groan of the wagon chassis broke the spell. Jude jumped to his feet, glancing behind him to see Ma had walked Fareed up the final slope. The torrent of rushing water was simply the old horse taking a leak. When he turned back to the woman, she'd disappeared.

"What's this?" demanded Ma, arms akimbo. She peered at him. "Something's happened." Her eyes scoured the highway. "What did you see? Dog pack? Meat-men? Come on! Come on! Out with it."

"A woman," Jude mumbled. "Over there, by those black trees. Floating. Wearing a dress the colour of sky. She was so ... so *beautiful*. And then, I saw ..." He faltered before the derision on Tattow's face. Summer gave a high-pitched giggle and clapped her hands, jigging from one foot to the other.

Ma snorted. "So where is she?" Jude didn't reply.

Osker regarded him with fever bright eyes, but Tattow laughed out loud. "If the lad's old enough for that sort of fantasy, he's certainly old enough for any task."

"She was real!" cried Jude. "I saw her. It wasn't imagination. I'd just finished doing The Road Thing." Ma scowled and gave him a small push.

"And who gave you leave?"

"I did it right. Seen it enough times."

"Let him alone," muttered Bett, hunkering down to spread the runes. "Crossroads means a reading. How else will we fix our direction?" She sniffed and wiped her nose on a fold of skirt. "Crossroads it is, and yet all I can see is an end to the road."

"Get on with it," snapped Ma. "Or I'll be pointing the way."

Jude remained standing, his gaze fixed on the yews. The buildings had gone; so had the crowd. There was still no sign of the woman but there were fat black corpsepeckers riding the wind currents far above. He shuddered. It had been a long time since they'd seen any birds and even the smallest was an omen of death, whether or not the cause of it. Now five, no, six were circling the crossroads: one for each of them. Nobody else noticed and Jude decided against pointing them out. Things were bad enough.

He turned towards the west. The heavy grey clouds had grown even larger, still denser, and seemed to be gnawing holes in the distant hills.

A fresh outbreak of bickering began.

"Wait up," muttered Betts, poring over the runes. "I see something else."

"No time," said Ma. "There's a real bad storm coming. Look later."

"It's important," insisted the feywoman. "Such things can't be hurried. I see what I see when I see it." She stared intently at Jude. "The sign is upon us."

"Important?" Ma's lip curled. "My stomach's empty. So is the boy's. That's what's important. We press on. We look for food. There'll be plenty of time for *signs* later, when we make camp for the night."

"Press on, is it? We go east, then, but let's hope you don't live to regret this noon." Bett sighed. She stood up slowly, replacing her rune stones in the little bag fastened with a yellow shell. "Or worse – die regretting it."

Summer whimpered and pulled at her tangled hair but Ma hesitated for less than a heartbeat.

"East it is," she announced. "Right, get up on the wagon, Jude."

"No." Jude shook his head. "I'll walk. It's Osker who needs to ride."

Ma glared, opened her mouth. And shut it again.

For once, she said nothing.

The highway wound through gentle valleys, running parallel to a wide river. Soon Jude began to recognise landmarks – a grooved hill shaped like an upturned arse, the lightning-blasted tree with brambles growing in its crown, a place where the road turned into its own twin – and before long it became apparent that they were approaching the red city. Ruined buildings sprouted from the earth. Progress slowed: their life revolved around the search for food and it was always worth investigating ancient gardens. In one, a few wizened crabs lay in the tangled grass and woody pipberries clustered along the hedge. There were roots too, rust-coloured, and only a little weevil-infested. Further on, Jude found a generous handful of raspberries and ate them secretly, squatting hidden among the thick canes. A mile or two later they came upon a walled enclosure where sparse heads of wheat struggled for life in an acre of shattered stone. He sat and watched – ignoring Tattow's sniping – as every last grain was gathered. It was something, but it was not enough for autumn was fast approaching and they'd built up no stores. Even Jude had come to understand that this was a winter they might not survive.

"The earth has turned against us," muttered Tattow. "She closes her hands and folds up her apron. Starvation is a bad way to die."

Summer began to keen, a high-pitched desolate sound that made a swathe of Jude's hair, nape to crown, tingle as it sprang erect. He covered his ears.

"Stop that!" commanded Ma, and jabbed Summer in the ribs. "There will be food in the city. Seek hard enough and there's always some sort of food to be found."

"These are the end days of the end days," said Bett, looking at the sky. "I too sense the earth growing weary. Her existence is a burden to her. Soon she will curl in on herself." She glared at Ma. "And all things will end unless there is one prepared to undertake what was always done and, in spite of long neglect, must be done again."

Ma ignored her, but Jude pricked up his ears. There it was again: the task. He sidled up to Bett but she turned her back and would not talk.

They stopped for the night in a meadow next to the river, where a stout stone bridge led through crumbling red-stone walls and up into the heart of the city.

Loosed from his harness, Fareed whickered and ripped at the lush grass while Summer danced away, gurgling with pleasure, to gather fragile flowers the colour of naked pink flesh from damp places beneath the trees. The rest of them foraged. Mushrooms gleamed white on a slope near the wood, which in turn yielded a little beech mast and a few handfuls of oak-corn. Herbs grew at the water's edge, mint, fennel, trailing nastsham with its bright orange flowers, and wild radish, the pungent root a forearm long and useful for driving off winter cold. Tattow dug for an hour or more with a sharpened stick before lifting it, all the while sweating and mouthing words that Jude had been clouted for uttering. There were fish in the river. Ma and Bett tied their skirts into knots and stood in the water, dragging nets finger-woven from stripped stingweed fibres against the current. They had no luck: the fish were wary and quick-flicked away from their long shadows and bony legs, but in the bank there were plenty of fat pink earthworms to set on skewers and roast with the mushrooms over a fire of pine cones gathered along the way.

As the food sizzled and popped, Bett cast and re-cast her runes, muttering to herself, her face growing steadily grimmer. She spoke to nobody, only snatched a few charred mushrooms from the flames, cramming them into her mouth before disappearing into the darkness.

"All the more for us," commented Tattow, with a shrug.

Most evenings were passed in story telling. Osker was the best weaver of tales; tonight he fell asleep before tasting a morsel of food. Ma silently passed his portion to Jude, but he was more interested in broaching the subject of the task.

"What did Osker mean? What do I have to do?"

"You would become a hero," said Tattow, and laughed aloud. "And high king for a ... "

"SILENCE!" roared Ma. "Tomorrow we must venture into the city to find winter stores. It'll be a hard day. Now we will sleep."

Tattow demurred. "Whatever the lad is ready to ask, he is ready to be told."

"Hold your tongue. You and your silly stories. I'll have none of that idle talk."

"Who are you to decide what I should and should not say?" demanded Tattow, extending his neck. He brandished one blue-patterned fist. "Carry on like this and you'll be travelling without me." Summer whimpered and he patted her hand, amending his threat to: "Without us."

"*I* am the mother," declared Ma, bringing her face close to his and grimacing horribly. "*I* am the bearer of the future. What I say goes." She lay down and turned away, pulling the blankets over her head. Tattow hawked and spat, angrily shaking off Summer who'd crept close for comfort.

Jude lay on his back, gazing upwards. The moon stared back at him, huge, bright orange and open-mouthed. He wondered what had happened to the storm and raised his head to stare towards the west. To his surprise the clouds were still there, standing out denser and blacker than the surrounding night sky. And, even more surprising, they were filled with stars, unfamiliar stars, too. Jude rubbed his eyes. That couldn't be right.

"Ma," he began.

"Sleep!"

Jude scowled. He curled over and began spinning his own stories, of difficult tasks, beautiful women – some naked – great rewards, and himself becoming a king.

When morning came they breakfasted on wheat soaked overnight and further softened in the embers. Since the others strapped on backpacks, Jude took one himself.

"I'm coming, too."

"You are not," said Ma, tucking a newly whetted blade into the top of her boot. "It'll be dangerous. Besides, someone must stay with Osker."

"Let Summer do it. What use would she be if there's any trouble?"

"She can carry her own weight if there's a finding." Ma scraped back her hair, working it into a mean plait. "Do as you're told. Get in the wagon. Now."

Jude stood his ground. "I am almost a man."

"You?" Ma gave him *the look*. He thought she might laugh in his face and quickly turned away to avoid further humiliation. Seeing one of the barrels empty, Jude carried it down to the river's edge and crouched on the pebbles filling it with the rush of living water. It would be needed later: Osker was constantly thirsty. A shadow fell on the river and he turned to see Bett had followed him. She was waiting when he climbed back up the bank.

"Bett," he mumbled, knowing she was the one person who might take his vision seriously and wishing he'd made more of an effort to seek her out. "I saw …"

But the old feywoman seemed in no mood to listen. One grubby hand impatiently flicked away his words. "Best you stay," she whispered, fixing him with her wild black eyes. "The time has come. The runes speak of great change, and night after night, in my dreams, I stand before the tree where the wolf howls and the skeleton dances." Bett hesitated. She looked away. "Last night, being full moon, I came to the river to seek guidance. I threw a yarrow molly into the black water and was granted a vision of the place."

"What place?"

"There is," Bett said, adopting a sing-song voice, "a green hill far away, without a city wall. That's where you must go."

It occurred to Jude that she was having one of her mad turns. They usually coincided with full moon. "We'll all go," he said, soothingly. Bett gave him an unexpectedly warm smile.

"Maybe. But if that was not to be, if all else fails, promise me, Jude, that you will shoulder your task. Promise me. Swear." She seized his arm, digging her bony fingers into his flesh. "Swear!"

"But I don't know what, or where – *Aw*!" The feywoman's hold tightened as Jude tried to pull free. By tomorrow there'd be a mass of bruises, elbow to wrist. Moon and stars help Bett if Ma caught sight of them. "Yes, yes, all right. I swear."

Bett gave a sigh of relief. Without another word she pressed her bag of runes into his hand and shambled away. He looked at it in surprise.

"We're off now," yelled Ma, shouldering her pack. "Get yourself back to the wagon and stay there." She gave Jude a rough hug and lowered her voice. "There's poppy tea if Osker's pain gets bad. Not too strong, mind, and not too much. That's got to last us until next flowering." The others lined up beside her.

"Wish us luck," said Tattow. He leered. "And lay off the fantasy women whilst we're gone. We wouldn't want a big strong lad like you spending all your time in your bunk. Fareed needs grooming and there's some holes in the canvas could do with patching."

Jude's face flamed. "Sharrup!" He shoved Bett's bag into a space high up in the wall of the wagon.

"Till later, then," said Ma and started to walk away. After a few paces, she seemed to change her mind and retraced her steps to hug him again. Then Summer danced up and pecked his cheek, making some of the high-pitched noises that were all she could manage by way of communication, and pressing a wilted fistful of the flowers that hung all round her into his hands. Such signs of affection were unusual. Jude felt a lump rise in his throat. He watched as the little party tramped across the open space and climbed up onto the bridge. When they returned, those packs should be weighed down with cans that would see them through the winter. There would be feasting tonight. His mouth watered in anticipation of sweet exotic fruits and savoury meat.

As soon as they'd disappeared from sight he turned his attention to Osker.

The sickness had eaten away at him, leaving his body frail as a skeleton leaf blown hither and thither by the winter wind. His skin was almost transparent now and Jude was sure he could see the blood coursing along his blue veins. Ma insisted he was improving by the day. Nobody believed it. Osker opened his eyes.

"Water," he whispered. Jude filled the little wooden bowl and held it to his pale lips. Osker slept for a while, waking when the sun was almost directly overhead. "Are they back?"

"Not yet."

Osker beckoned him closer. "Your task ..." he breathed.

"Yes?" Jude knelt down, hardly able to disguise his impatience at the ensuing silence. He cleared his throat. Osker didn't respond. He touched his shoulder. "Osker, tell me what I'm supposed to do."

"Are they back?"

Jude shook his head. "Not yet."

"Water." He drank a little. And slept again. This time when he woke, the light was dying and Jude had been backwards and forwards, wagon to bridge, watching anxiously for the first glimpse of Ma and the others. "Are they back?" Jude shook his head. A terrible fear clutched at his heart. As if sensing it, Osker clutched at his hand. "You are a man now, Jude. Whatever happens, you must continue." He stopped to catch his breath. "I see your path with my inner eye – make for the rising sun, stop for nothing, neither fear, nor sorrow, hunger, nor thirst. You will come to a great river close by a yellow building topped by four spires. From there, head south. After many days, you will see from afar a hill surrounded by water."

"What then?" gulped Jude, gnawing at his fist.

"Not alone. Help will come. You will not be alone." Osker spoke no more. Night fell and his harsh breathing punctuated the darkness. When it stopped, Jude turned his face to the canvas and wept.

In the grey dawn, Jude returned to the bridge. Nothing stirred along the length of the street. A tall bruised-purple tower, rising over both trees and broken chimneys watched him through its many eyes. A small wind moaned and sighed through the reeds at the water's edge. Jude wept some more.

After a while he knuckled his eyes and wiped his nose on his sleeve. Squatting here wasn't going to solve anything. The fools had probably got lost. Or they'd struck lucky and were arguing over the most sensible way to get a huge stash of food back to the wagon. The best course of action would be to go into the city and find them. This thought cheered him considerably. Then he remembered Osker.

It was a fundamental rule of life that – hunger being what it was – the dead must be disposed of quickly. Immediate burial was out of the question: when Da died it took everyone in the group a day and a night of digging to hollow a suitably sized final bed from the hard earth, therefore the leave-taking would have to wait until the others returned. On the other hand, what if something should savage Osker's body whilst he was away?

Jude returned to the camp site and chewed on a handful of wheat while racking his brain for another solution. Kicking apart the dead fire provided it. Years ago, the group had been much larger with six wagons, possibly more – his memory of it had grown dim – travelling in convey backwards and forwards along the edges of the mountains waiting for a sign. He'd never been told why so many people died so quickly, but he remembered the leaping flames as the bodies were burned in their wagons together with every last possession. It was necessary, said Ma. Jude chewed harder and spat husk. He couldn't do that here – wasn't Osker's wagon, for a start – and even if he gathered enough wood to burn him on the open ground, a fire of that size would draw too much attention. They might return to find both wagon and Fareed gone.

Inspiration finally came from one of Osker's own stories: as if for a hero, Jude would build a floating pyre and send it towards the western sea. With any luck it should arrive there at the same time as the setting sun.

There was still the problem of touching it. The body. Dead.

Jude walked up and down for a long time before Osker's words again rescued him. He was not a coward. He would do what must be done.

Osker weighed next to nothing, but he was tall and an awkward burden. After wrapping him in his blanket, Jude somehow got the bundle outside and laid it on the ground with as much reverence as could be managed. Then he dragged his sleeping board out of the wagon, rolled Osker's body onto it, and arranged his few possessions around him. After a moment's thought, he added the little wooden drinking bowl. It was not really Osker's, very much

Ma's, and a treasured love gift too – Da hollowed it from a knot of oak years ago and spent many long evenings decorating it with an intricate design of leaves and oak-corn – but Jude had no other way of honouring the man or the moment. Perhaps she'd understand. Bent double, puffing and straining, Jude hauled the board to the water's edge and piled it with the entire winter supply of fir cones. There was no kindling, but a mound of tinder-dry leaves served. Greedy as ever, the river snatched the board and began nudging it downstream so that Jude had to plunge in and wade after it, holding the flint above his head, struggling to keep the board steady and coax a flame from the leaves at the same time. Leaves to pine cones to blanket, the fire finally caught; a small wind fanned the flames, drawing them man-high as the pyre rounded a bend in the river and disappeared.

After wringing the worst of the water from his clothes, Jude caught Fareed and spent some time hobbling and staking him within a thicket of trees. The wagon he left where it was. Tattow had made sure it couldn't be seen by anyone passing by. His wet boots rubbed at his ankles as he began the ascent, bent low, sneaking doorway to doorway up the long stretch of highway.

Twilight gathered and still Jude could find no trace of Ma or the others.

The wind was growing in strength now: it whistled along the gappy eaves of buildings and set sheets of metal flapping against walls like slow handclaps; it created pillars of white dust and made them dance themselves out of existence; it sent down roof tiles to skim the air above his head. Parts of this small city seemed familiar. Jude knew he'd been brought here before, but twice he lost himself in the same spider's web of tiny alleyways and he could find none of the places where Ma might have gone to search for food.

Finally the light grew so dim that Jude knew he must seek shelter for the night.

He was unwilling to return to the wagon, the thought of its emptiness appalled him, and anyway, to do so would mean braving that open stretch of highway again tomorrow. Nearby stood a massive building surmounted by the tall tower that had watched him earlier and from which stone fingers pointed towards the sky.

Jude kept his distance. It had many doors, all wide and barred with metal, stone monsters snarled from the roof, every one of the arched porches was crammed with goblin shadows, and anything could be hiding behind the crumbling buttresses.

There was a smaller building opposite, fashioned from bruised-purple stone. One half of its double door – set back between pillars – was slightly ajar. Jude pushed it open and listened intently. Silence. The floor was covered by thick dust; nothing living had crossed it recently. There was a second set of doors a few paces further in, and as Jude slid between them he recognised the great room beyond. It was full of books. They'd all been here several autumns back – he remembered Osker handling the volumes with reverence, speaking in a strange rhythmic voice as he ran his finger along the lines of runes and pointed to the illustrations, but Tattow had shown him how to line his boots with the pages and Ma had filled her pack with torn off covers that made fire building an easy thing for many weeks. Jude took an armful of books and leafed through them in the last of the light, closely inspecting any depictions that might be ancient kings but letting those without pictures tumble onto the floor.

By now he was really hungry and cursing himself for not having the wit to bring a pocketful of wheat with him. Without water, the paper was uneatable. His tongue stuck to the roof of his mouth. In the end he curled beneath a table and tried to sleep.

Towards dawn, Jude was woken by an almighty crash.

He sat up quickly, banging his head, his mouth even drier and his heart pounding as he struggled to remember where he was and why he was there while the echoes of a massive fall continued to rumble round the building. Then came another crash, this one even louder, followed by a sharp tinkling sound close by. Jude sat quite still, breathing quietly and hugging his knees, waiting for sun-up. The first grey light showed that the remaining window had imploded, littering the floor with glass shards. They looked useful. Jude selected the most lethal looking, cutting his fingers in the process. He bound the wounds with many strips of paper and peed over them in an attempt to disguise the smell of blood.

Outside, the world had changed. Half of the building opposite had fallen, leaving a gaping cavern full of tall columns.

Surprisingly, apart from the pile of massive stone blocks at one side that must have been responsible for last night's noise, there was little masonry to mark its collapse. Instead a gaping space in the earth had opened, darker than the darkest winter night, not a pit exactly – for it had no bottom and no proper sides, and its rim was not solid, it wavered, like black water without being wet, or like dark cloud, yet without air – but more like something from a dream that had ceased being. Jude backed away and stopped trying to make sense of it. *A hole* was the only way he could think about this lack of place, and that was the end of it.

For a moment, he stood irresolute, wondering which part of the city to search first. A little rain fell and he threw back his head to catch the drops. Then, squaring his shoulders, Jude set off and deliberately turned down the grimmest of all the grim passages.

And there in front of him was the woman, smiling, beckoning, and retreating rapidly. Today she was clothed in ocean – blues and deep greens shot through with emerald, moody greys, purple – that shifted and intermingled, rippled, undulated round her body. A circlet of fan-shaped shells held back her hair; there were more shells at her wrist and neck. This time, Jude fought off his terror and ran after her, eyes fixed on her beautiful breasts beneath the ebb and flow of colour – fighting all the while against another vision of the great open square with its milling crowds that repeatedly superimposed itself on his surroundings – and she led him deeper and deeper through blackened alleys that twisted and turned, across a space pitted by dark pools streaked with drowned rainbows, under an arch, up steps and down again, until he found himself breathless and alone next to a tight cluster of gutted houses.

Jude's heart sank. She'd disappeared.

In that same moment he heard shouts and rough laughter. The air was permeated with the tantalising smell of roasting meat. Flattening himself against broken walls, crouching and flitting silently between piles of bricks, Jude edged nearer. The noise grew louder. It became the sound of fighting. Someone yelled. Another voice cursed. There followed the clash of metal on metal, and a terrible howl followed by silence. Jude's way was blocked by a solid wall, but there were gaps in the brickwork and, seizing a jag of metal, he crumbled away the mortar until he'd made a thumb-sized hole. Peering through, he made out a small courtyard partially roofed with rags heaped over diagonally laid timbers, and within which four men lay sprawled upon the ground. The fire was out of his range of vision, but Jude could smell burning flesh now and hear the pop and crackle of fat dripping onto flames. There was a great deal of blood around.

These were undoubtedly meat-men. This was dangerous stuff. Bett said they could smell living flesh a mile off.

Jude was about to back silently away when a small movement on the far side of the yard caught his eye. He stopped.

For the second time, what he *thought* he was seeing wasn't possible. He pinched himself and looked again. No mistake. A boy of his own age, smaller, perhaps a little younger, thin, filthy and half-clothed, had been tied by the hands to a metal ring set into a post.

Once, long ago, Tattow had kicked the mounting block from beneath his feet as Jude was trying to climb into the wagon, and that was exactly as he felt now. Ma repeatedly proclaimed that he was the last child, more precious than life itself, but it wasn't true because he was looking at another, a captive, moreover. There'd been no cosseting here. This boy had a black eye and a bloody mouth. He was struggling so hard to free himself that there were raw rope burns around both wrists.

A rescuer was needed, another hero out of one of Osker's tales; Tattow would do, Ma even, but where were they? There was no one here but himself. And what could he do? Jude watched for a while longer.

The nearest man rolled over and sat up, holding his head and groaning. His face was pitted and scarred. He had no ears, but his nose was long and sharp. He sniffed the air, clambered awkwardly to his feet and stared fixedly at the place where Jude cowered, trembling. Then one of his comrades, a thick-set man in a coat of dappled hides roughly stitched and fringed with long whippy tails, reached out and seized his ankles, pulling them from under him, so that the man with no ears toppled like an uprooted tree, breath knocked out of him one end and a mighty fart the other. His comrades sat up, roaring with laughter and began passing a skin bottle between them. No-ears cursed and grunted. Seizing a length of timber he levered himself upright and proceeded to lay about him, clouting two of the men on the backs of their heads before they got wind of his intention, striking so hard that they collapsed insensible again. Dappled-skin saw: ducking the blow aimed at him, he ran forward, baring his teeth, growling like a cornered dog, and butted No-ears full in the face. They both went down.

A flicker of sea-green fabric appeared at the corner of the shelter, the suggestion of red-gold hair, and of a heartbreakingly beautiful smile that hung on the air – and swiftly faded. The roar of an invisible crowd hovered like an echo of some distant memory. The stench of forgotten shame rose to coil, adder-crazy, round him.

Something happened to Jude. His blood seemed to boil in his veins. Without stopping to think, he ran along the wall and came to a ragged opening that had once been a window. Signalling the boy to silence, he clambered through and, taking out the largest of his glass shards, crept behind the supine figures. He sawed frantically at the rope, soaking it with his own blood. No-ears began to twitch; one hand roamed across the ground, blindly seeking his club. Sweat ran down Jude's forehead, misting his eyes, his heart became a clenched fist thumping against his ribs, but still he continued to saw. No-ears' fingers closed on the club; he grunted. The boy strained his hands apart increasing the rope's tension. Jude sawed faster. The rope began to fray. A minute later the small captive was free. There was no time for thanks. Already Dappled-skin was wiping the blood from his closed eyes.

"Bluddy run for yer life!" hissed the boy.

# 2

They ran blind, slipping, sliding, crashing into buildings, bumping into each other, stumbling over rubble, squeezing through gaps, cramming their bodies through the tiniest of openings, inching along the narrowest alleys – obeying an instinct screaming that smaller size might be their only advantage – and expecting at any moment to hear the thud thud thud of feet behind them. Jude's terror was heightened by the fevered images continually thrusting themselves before his eyes, turning the headlong flight into a battle in which he threshed the air as he fought against the tightly packed crowd heaving forward to engage with unseen assailants. The black clad figures on their glossy horses closed in. The howls inside his head grew louder. Where water poured from a shattered pipe, Jude thrust aside fear of it becoming a punishing jet aimed at his chest, marking time only long enough to swill the worst of the tracking-scent gore from his hands. His vision abruptly cleared. They ran again. Suddenly the great tower loomed beyond a broken wall and Jude grabbed the boy's arm and pointed, too breathless to explain.

Emerging onto the highway, Jude saw that more of the tower had disappeared without trace. Not a scrap of fallen masonry remained. The *hole* had grown. In a couple of hours it had ingested most of the green space immediately in front of the building, including a vertical slice of one of the trees. From the corner of his eye, still moving fast, Jude saw the rest of the trunk cease to be, silently erased like a dirty mark on the skin, and was almost sure that the topmost branches remained hanging in mid-air a few seconds after their support had gone. The nothingness was hungry. Perhaps soon it would take the entire city. Jude kept his distance.

And there was the hill down to the river.

"This way!" croaked Jude.

Ditching all caution, they galloped straight down the middle – not daring to look back, not caring what eyes watched from the ruined buildings – stumbled over the end of the bridge and raced as one over the open grass, making for the deep shadow beneath the nearest trees. Jude had been praying that the others would be waiting, but they were not. Neither was there any sign of Fareed, though he was sure the hobbling and staking had been properly done. Fresh waves of panic broke over him. Without Fareed they were finished. He battered his way through trailing branches and, a few moments later, found the horse calmly nipping at greenery. Fareed had slipped his hobble and uprooted the stake. From now on he'd have to be far more careful. Jude bent double, knuckling the stitch in his side and panting. The boy, who wasn't even out of breath, stood poised for further flight, staring curiously at him.

"Why you stopping?"

Still puffing and blowing, Jude nodded to the wagon.

"So?"

"That's home. Shelter. Our horse can pull it. He'll walk farther than we can."

For a moment, the boy looked unconvinced. Then he nodded. "What we waiting for? Let's get going."

"Yeh, right. Let me just …" Jude took a stick and carefully checked that nothing had crawled under the canvas in his absence. This was really Tattow's job. "What's your name?"

"Kid." The boy was in a half crouch, staring over his shoulder. "They called me Kid. How bluddy long's all this going to take?"

"Not long." He would prepare for a quick get-away. Everything must be done properly. Jude led the horse to the river and let him drink his fill. "I'm Jude," he said, finally, when it became apparent Kid wasn't going to reciprocate. He carefully backed Fareed between the shafts, racking his brains to remember what went where, easing on the collar, tightening the girth and the breeching strap, checking and rechecking that everything had been done correctly.

"What you fiddling about with now?" demanded Kid. "Come on, we got to get out of here. We ain't got much time. That one with no ears – see the nose on him? He can track down anything."

Jude inspected Fareed's hooves. "I'm getting everything ready, but we can't leave without the others. We'll be off the minute they come. They shouldn't be long now – went to find food and they've been gone nearly three days already. That's who I was looking for when I found you."

"Oh." Kid looked at his feet. There was a long silence. "Would that be three old women and a man with blue pictures all over his arms and back?"

A cold sick terror descended on Jude. He felt his bowels churn and looked towards the bushes. His lips trembled and there was nothing he could do to stop them. "Yeh, Ma, Bett, Summer, and Tattow."

"No good waiting for them," said Kid. "They won't come." He was still for a moment, squinting at Jude through his fringe of matted hair. "Think about them later. We got to go."

"What happened to them?"

Kid shook his head. "I ain't telling you. All you need to know is they're gone. Now, let's go."

"Go? Go where?"

"Don't matter. Anywhere. The farther we go the better. Unless you want to end up like them. Come on, whatever your name is, shift your arse. We got to move now, straight away."

"All right," said Jude, numb with misery. He wiped his eyes. What did it matter where they went? What did anything matter?

Head down, he guided Fareed back onto the highway, hardly bothering with The Road Thing beyond one quick look up towards the tower, and started to plod roughly westwards, retracing their route of three days ago. The watery sun had just tipped over the zenith. There was a nip in the air. A gust of wind tore a scatter of leaves from the trees. This was the weather for a big fire in a secure hollow. Wrapped in his blankets, his stomach full of baked roots and roasted jessnuts, he'd lie dozing and listening to each of them tell stories so familiar that he knew the ending almost as soon as the first few words were out – Ma always went on about how much better everything was in the Good Old Days, Bett told tales of devils and angels, fire and floods, dying and becoming young again, heroes venturing into the labrynthian underworld to retrieve lost treasure, long ago things before the beginning of time, whilst Tattow concentrated blow by blow, thrust by thrust on epic battles. Osker's stories were the best though. They drew you inside, until you could almost smell and taste the lavish banquets, see the gleam of gold, the sparkle of gems, and hear the clash of duelling swords, the song of the harp. But all that was done with. There would be no more stories.

Kid darted ahead, peered round a corner and sprinted back. "Can't he go no bluddy faster?" And when Jude hunched over and weeping again didn't answer, yelled: "Want me to tell you what they'll do when they catch you?"

"Leave me alone."

"Get a bluddy move on, can't you?"

"I said, LEAVE ME ALONE."

"All right, I will." Kid looked towards a distant wood. "I'm off. I ain't sticking around to watch them skin you alive." He began scrambling over the wall at the side of the highway. "Bye, then. Thanks for cutting me free."

"No! Wait!" Jude scrubbed at his face and sniffed loudly. "Don't go. Please." The last thing he wanted was to be left on his own. There'd be time later to grieve over Ma and the others. Kid was right: the most important thing was to get as far away from this place as quickly as possible. Besides, getting caught by No-ears wasn't going to bring any of them back. "Yeh, he can go faster." He climbed up onto the box and leaned out, extending his hand. "Jump up." Kid's hand was icy, and so small and claw-like that he could feel the individual bones. It was also covered with inflamed insect bites and Jude let go quickly, rubbing his own hand vigorously against the canvas. Reaching down the switch he tapped Fareed lightly on the flank. The horse snorted and tossed his mane, but increased his pace so marginally that they were moving very little faster than walking speed.

"Give him a bluddy big whack on the arse," suggested Kid.

Jude shook his head. "I can't do that. This is an old horse. He's got to be treated with respect. If anything happens to Fareed we're sunk."

"Yeh and anything happens to us he'll be chunks of meat roasting over a fire straight after they've finished gnawing on you." Kid snatched the switch and gave the horse an almighty blow on the croup. Fareed whinnied and broke into a trot. "Now he understands, see?"

"Give me that." Jude grabbed at the switch and scowled, regretting the impulse to call Kid back. He was pleased to see that Fareed was already slowing down. "Don't ever do that again – you hear me? This ain't your horse."

Kid shrugged. He sniffed the air. The wind was growing stronger. It ruffled their hair and made their eyes stream. More leaves were falling, together with scatters of nuts that they daren't stop to harvest. Loose ends of canvas billowed and snapped as they tugged at the woven hazel framework roofing the wagon.

"We ought to change direction. Wind's in our face." Kid fidgeted and looked back down the road. "That means it'll be carrying our smell towards *them*."

"Fareed can turn off the highway soon as we get clear of the buildings. No good going down any of these tracks. Most of them will be blocked by rubble." Jude looked up at the sky, noting that leaden clouds still hung over the distant hills. He frowned. What sort of clouds didn't move for days at a time? "By the look of it there's a massive storm brewing – at least that should put No-ears off the scent – but those clouds have been gathering for days and it hasn't come to anything yet."

"Still bluddy cold," said Kid, and shivered.

Jude nodded to a wicker hamper. "Spare clothes in there."

"And I'm hungry," said Kid, pulling on a woollen tunic made by Ma and that Jude had long outgrown.

"There's wheat in that sack."

"How come you're so fat?" asked Kid, through a mouthful of grain.

"How come you're skinny?" retorted Jude.

"I ain't never in my life seen anybody fat as you before." Kid sniffed. "And why's your hair that funny colour?"

Jude looked at him in astonishment. "It's red. What's wrong with that? Talking about hair, why you keep all those bugs running round in yours?"

"I like 'em." Kid obligingly scratched at his scalp.

They continued in silence until the wagon rattled past the place where the group had harvested the very wheat that they were now both chewing. Before long, Jude thought, they'd reach the double road, then the lightning-blackened tree with its green bramble hair, the bum hill, and, long before nightfall, the yew trees where the woman had first shown herself to him. The safest thing might be to turn off the highway there. At least the track was sheltered and the fast flowing stream at the bottom would wash away their scent. Having made the decision, Jude immediately began to feel uncomfortable, and vaguely guilty. *Make for the rising sun*, Osker had said. *You will come to a great river close by a yellow building of tall spires. From there, head south.* And Bett, hadn't he promised her that he'd carry out his task? If they were all dead, it was the least he could do in their memory, but how could he even try when they were going the wrong way. Jude stopped the wagon. Fareed stamped and blew, his breath rising in coils on the cold air.

Kid pulled the tunic from over his nose and mouth. "What's up?"

"I must go east."

"Yeh. Right. Bluddy brilliant idea." Kid took another handful of wheat. "East is behind us. Back through the city."

"Then that's where I'm going." Jude pulled Fareed's head round, turning the wagon to face the way they'd just come.

"WHAT YOU BLUDDY DOING?" screamed Kid. "They'll catch us. They kill for fun. They pull people apart. They cook and eat bits of you in front of your eyes."

"Then we'll have to move very fast." Jude remembered the way eastwards now: the highway heading into the rising sun on a cool spring morning; his young self wrapped in a blanket, squashed between Ma and Da.

"No!" Kid threw himself forward and yanked on the ropes. "Are you bluddy mad? You can't!"

Jude didn't answer, for there was the woman, this time dressed in a field of flowers. With every movement, blossoms shifted and rippled, spring to summer to autumn, tight bud to full blow to bud again, on a background of constantly changing greens. Her head was wreathed with more flowers. An aura of delicately coloured petals surrounded her and a sweet fragrance drifted towards him. She was more beautiful than ever. She smiled. She beckoned.

"Get out if you want," said Jude, hoarsely, his whole being longing for he hardly knew what. "I'm going on. I know this is the right way now." He glanced at Kid, but the boy didn't answer. His mouth was wide open, so were his eyes. "You can see her, too?"

The woman was already fading rapidly, and yet something of her remained, like the pale twin of a rainbow, almost but not quite there, hanging in the air above the highway, always a little way ahead. Keeping his eyes fixed on that spot, Jude reached for the switch but Fareed was already picking up speed, breaking into such a brisk trot that he might have had eight legs rather than four and they covered the distance in an unbelievably short time. The mist of colours danced ahead of them and onto the bridge, whereupon Fareed broke into a canter, wagon swaying violently, creaking and graunching, all the carefully stowed baskets and hampers, pans and utensils breaking free with a clang and a clatter, tipping from side to side and bouncing off the canvas. Up the hill they went at a gallop. As they came onto the flat, both barrels propped behind the seat tipped over with a mighty whoosh, soaking the boys' backs with ice cold water. Jude yelled with shock, half turned in his seat and, receiving a further slop of water centre chest, was immediately back in the square, fighting to escape from the mêlée. A flailing arm struck his head. He was down, lying on cold grey slabs, staring up at the sliver of grey sky. The ropes slipped from his hands. Jerked back to reality, Jude clung to the seat for dear life as Fareed narrowly missed the gaping chasm that had already eaten away half of the highway. Ears back, mouth gaping, the horse swung the wagon to the right and stormed straight across the market square, weaving between rust wrecks and the line of ancient gibbets.

As if in the worst of nightmares, Jude was suddenly aware of No-ears and the other one – Dappled-skin – running parallel with them, keeping pace, edging nearer; nearer still. And now he saw the other two on the far side of the square, racing to stop the wagon by shoving mangled rust wrecks across the main exit. Kid began screaming a forbidden word over and over again. No-ears was gaining; his monstrous face was only a few paces away. Something, a long knife, glanced off the curved frame and clattered against the cobbles. Jude flung himself backwards as another blade plunged into Fareed's shoulder. Blood fountained. Fareed rolled his eyes and ran faster, so fast that for a while the wagon slewed sideways and was dragged after him on a single pair of wheels. Jude held tight and waited to die. He closed his eyes. The alternative was no better: he was still on the ground, kicked and buffeted; a large boot narrowly missed his hand. The horse whinnied. A huge crash and a scraping of metal followed and he opened his eyes to find Fareed charging the barrier, shunting the rust wrecks before him. Voices bellowed instructions. Projectiles battered the canvas. Numb with terror, Jude wrapped his arms round his head. And found himself doing the same, on the ground, confronted by a veritable forest of forward marching legs. This time the bumps and blows seemed preferable to reality.

Gradually the horse slowed down. When he plucked up enough courage to look, Jude found they had left the city and were travelling along a wider highway. Already the ruins were giving way to wasteland dotted with stunted trees. Kid was inching along Fareed's back, reaching out to get hold of the trailing ropes.

It was over. Jude's gut churned. He heaved and leaned over the side of the wagon as the chewed-up wheat erupted from his mouth leaving a foul taste on his tongue. Letting Kid manage the horse as best he could, Jude went in search of one of the wizened apples Ma had carefully hidden away. Black misery overwhelmed him at the sight of her jumbled possessions, everything turned upside down, just like his life. He was alone. Osker had promised he wouldn't be, he'd had a vision just before dying, but it must have been Kid he'd glimpsed, and what use was he? Jude bit into the sour fruit and wept. Then he remembered the woman and brightened a little.

When he climbed back outside, Fareed was trotting along at a brisk pace. His head was up and he lifted his feet higher than in Jude's memory. The horse had become sprightly. He looked ... *purposeful.* As for Kid, he was whistling between his teeth and playing scrat's-cradle with a length of Ma's twine looped around his fingers. He shifted along the seat. "Heard you spewing your guts up. All right, are you? Who was that woman? Where'd she go?"

"Don't know. That's three times she's, you know, suddenly appeared out of nowhere. She's never said anything." Perhaps she was mute, like poor Summer. Jude recalled Bett's stories. "D'you reckon she might be an angel?"

"A what?"

"Angel. In the old days they brought messages."

"Who from?" demanded Kid, looking at him askance. "And where are they?"

"Don't know," admitted Jude, annoyed by Kid's sneer. "If I see her again, I'll ask her. *All right*?"

"Yeh, keep your red hair on." Kid sniffed. "What now?"

"We go in search of a green hill."

"No bluddy shortage of those," said Kid, pointing.

Jude followed his finger. There were indeed many hills. His eye was drawn to a rounded one not too far away, topped with a knot of fir trees, forming a dark crown. Maybe a dozen ancient tracks converged on the spinney, but as the highway curved near enough to see the hill in its entirety it became obvious that there was something wrong with its far side. He rubbed his eyes. Instead of smooth slope, he could see one shoulder was dramatically concave – almost as if something had taken a huge bite out of it – and there was nothing inside that dark bite, nothing at all, nothing, not even a shadowy view of the countryside behind, even though he could quite clearly see woods and hills in the far distance. It didn't make sense. Jude stopped looking.

"The hill we want is far away, in a place where there's a lot of water."

"How much water?"

"A lot."

"How far away?"

"Dunno."

"Half a day? Day?"

Jude sighed. "I *don't know*. All right?"

"Why you going there anyway?"

"I promised."

"Who?"

Jude glared. "Somebody. I'm going for my group, right? You don't have to." He waited anxiously to see what the other boy would do and breathed a low sigh of relief when he seemed in no hurry to leave. Neither spoke for a while.

"They will come after us," said Kid, finally. "They won't give up."

"Why?"

"They'll want me back."

"Why?" Jude looked Kid up and down. There was no meat on him.

Kid didn't answer. The wind changed direction and turned lazy, trying to blow straight through them, rather than go round, and Jude shivered, only now really aware of his wet back.

"Let's stop and find some dry clothes. No point in dying of cold when we got all that stuff in the back." Stuff, Jude realised, with a pang, that its owners no longer had any use for. He scrambled over the scattered hampers, pulling out this and that in the search for warm woollens. Kid took Summer's tunic and

Tattow's thick bracken-coloured jacket and patched grey trousers without a word, carrying them off to change in what little privacy was afforded behind the wagon. Such modesty was unusual. Jude peered through a chink in the canvas and caught a glimpse of grimy back and skinny shoulders covered with cuts and bruises. He heard Kid cry out as his rags pulled off fresh scabs. Ashamed, Jude stepped back and, after finding clothes for himself, made a feeble attempt at restoring order whilst searching for something to put on Fareed's cut. There were a great many pots in Bett's healing bag. Apart from poppy tea, he didn't know what any of the powders and potions would do and bitterly regretted never learning. All he could do was use the remaining drops of water to clean the gaping wound and lay a dock leaf over the place. It needed a couple of stitches but Jude lacked the courage.

"We'd better move on," said Kid, reappearing with both sleeves and trouser legs rolled up many times. He broke off some more of the twine and tied his jacket at the waist. Jude wanted to laugh. The clothes were so much too big and bundled that the boy looked as round as a kickabout ball.

Kid caught his eye. "At least I'm bluddy warm now."

"What happened to you then?" asked Jude, as with a dramatic tossing of the mane, Fareed set off again. "How did you end up with those meat-men? Where's your group?"

Kid shrugged. "Doesn't matter."

"I told you about mine," Jude said, plaintively

"Doesn't matter," Kid repeated. "There's nothing much to tell. It was so long ago I can't even remember my real folk properly. Maybe they're dead. There was a lot of fighting when I was taken. Happens every time." He turned his face away.

"Every time?" Jude stared, horrified. "You mean …?"

"Never mind all that past stuff. It's this last lot you ought to be worrying about. They were five against ten fighting the group what had me before – one of them got his throat cut and his guts hooked out, that was the end of him – and yet they still won. Yan got his nose slit. Another lost two fingers. They won't give up easy. I keep telling you – they'll come after us."

"It's getting dark," observed Jude. The light was thickening. Already the trees were blurring into patches of darkness. A silvery mist hovered over the grasslands. Looking up, he found the first star. He risked a quick look at the motionless storm clouds and found they'd doubled in size. Their tops had become smooth and domed. Perhaps it meant early snow.

"Near enough full moon tonight," said Kid, back to twisting the twine into loops and diamonds round his fingers. "Let's hope there's enough light to keep going. Like I said, further we get from them, the better chance we've got."

He said nothing for a while, and Jude was quiet, too. There was so much to think about. Would things have been different if he'd insisted on accompanying Ma into the city? Had Bett foreseen disaster? Who was the beautiful woman if she wasn't an angel, and why did she disappear? Was she the bringer of the terrible pictures inside his head? And the task – what was the nature of the task? He ran through the most colourful of Osker's stories until the uneven surface of the highway jolted him out of his musings. The black crust was badly broken here; small shrubs had pushed through its surface and they clattered against the wagon's under-chassis.

The moon was lying low on the horizon, bathing the landscape in a murky grey light. They were approaching a crossroads, and Jude wondered about stopping for The Road Thing, but Fareed suddenly put on speed and it seemed more trouble that it was worth when the worst of any danger was probably following them. Beyond the cross a stand of trees cast long shadows that seemed to reach for them. Something moved. Jude peered into the darkness. He nudged Kid.

"You see anything?"

"Nah, I ain't scared of shadows – *bluddy yes!*"

A large figure had stepped from under the trees and was now standing right in the middle of the highway. Fareed stopped reluctantly and only when both Kid and Jude pulled on the ropes with all their strength. The horse pawed at the ground. His flanks quivered. He snorted and blew.

"Is that one of them?" Exertion had brought them closer together and Jude could feel Kid trembling.

"Don't know. I can't see."

"Hold tight," whispered Jude. "We're going to charge straight at him. He'll soon move. And if he don't get out of the way, too bad, he'll get knocked down."

Jude took a deep breath, tapped Fareed's rump and flicked the ropes slack. Immediately, the horse leapt forward. Within seconds they could see enough to know that this was not one of the red city's meat-men, in spite of the wide hat pulled well down and casting further shadow over his face. He was taller than any of them, broad at the shoulder, majestic in bearing. His blue coat was long, cloak-like, scuffing the dust. One hand clutched a large knobbled staff and he held this out as the wagon approached, obstructing even more of the way. *Stop for nothing*, Osker had said. It seemed an excellent idea. Jude yanked the left rope hard, guiding Fareed to the side of the highway, almost in the ditch; he touched him again with the switch, urging him on. They were almost level with the man now, near enough to see the pale gleam of an eye. He wasn't moving. He continued to stand right in Fareed's path. Jude's heart began hammering against his ribs. Another minute and the stranger would be under the wheels, crushed and broken.

But Fareed stopped dead.

"MOVE! MOVE!" yelled Jude, desperately bringing down the switch. Fareed snorted. He stamped a fore foot. Jude hit him again. And again. Nothing happened. And suddenly the man was sitting beside him, bringing with him the smell of the high moors – bracken, heather, pine resin – overlaid with that of burned wood and the faintest tang of sulphur.

"You took your time, boy."

"W-w-what?" stammered Jude. Fareed was already moving again. How was he to get rid of this fellow?

"I've been waiting here for three long days."

"I-I d-don't know where you're g-going, but you can't come with us. I've a task to carry out."

"Indeed you have."

"G-get out! G-go on! P-p-please let us go!"

A big gnarled hand patted Jude's knee. "You can't do without me, boy. I know the way." He laughed uproariously, a great booming sound, reminiscent of distant thunder. "And more than that, I know what's at the heart of the matter."

"Who are you?"

"You may call me Tyrod." Tyrod pushed back his hat revealing a strong, grim face with heavy eyebrows and a long grey beard.

Jude saw to his horror that one of the man's eyes was blind, off-white and slightly wrinkled, looking exactly like a solitary snake's egg. Tyrod leaned round him to peer at Kid. "Ah. So you're the other one? Dear me. Dear me. Well, well, I dare say by and by everything will become clear." He laughed again, but stopped abruptly. "No need to look so frightened. I'm here to protect you both. And now …" He held out his arms.

Down from the bleached-bone skeleton of a tree flapped two glossy birds, plumage gleaming like deep water in the moonlight, black as corpsepeckers but far larger, with wingspans almost as wide as the wagon. Jude shrank back as the creatures alighted on the roof with perfectly synchronised thumps. Birds were evil, and these birds were probably more evil than most, for they regarded him arrogantly, full on and not first with one side of the head then the other like the rest of their kind. Tyrod reached up a knot-veined hand and sleeked the feathers of each in turn, but the other hand lay quiescent in his lap, and Jude thought he caught a faint glint of silver as moonlight played over the fingers. The birds bowed and danced, shifting their weight from foot to foot. After a brief hesitation, Kid stood up and held out one scabby palm full of wheat, which the creatures snapped their beaks and jostled for.

Jude shuddered and pulled at Kid's arm. "Leave them alone. They bring sickness and death."

"How so?" enquired Tyrod, his lips twitching with amusement.

"All birds do. Everyone knows that. What do you think happened to all the people who lived in these parts long ago? There used to be as many birds then as there are stars in the sky. They wanted the earth for themselves, so there was a great battle in which they rained down sickness from above. You know what they say about birds: *one for sorrow, two for pain, three for sickness, four for wane, five for fever, six for cold, and seven for a wasting never to be cured.* Only good bird is a dead bird and even then you got to be careful."

"Ah," nodded Tyrod, "that would explain why these two bear the names Doom and Destruction."

"Yes," said Jude, uncomfortably aware of being laughed at. "And they ain't riding up there."

"Don't worry, boy. They'll be off come morning."

"Shhh!" hissed Kid. "Listen!"

At first there was nothing except the brisk clip of Fareed's hooves, the querulous creak of branches in an ancient tree, the long-drawn-out call of a far away night howl, and then Jude picked up a faint noise, little more than a vibration, in the distance. It sounded no more threatening than a web-trapped bee, and yet the hair at his nape prickled and stood on end.

"Rust wreck?" He looked at the pale blur of Kid's face in the moonlight.

The question hardly needed asking. Minute by minute the sound grew louder, closer, until they could clearly make out the low growl and sharp pop-pop-pop of a rust wreck brought to life.

"It's them. They're catching up with us," said Kid, and sprang upright as if preparing to leap from the wagon. The great birds shuffled and clacked an alarm.

Tyrod grabbed at Kid's bulky jacket. "No need for that. Wait." He looked up at the moon and muttered something under his breath. And immediately, long rags of progressively darker cloud began to form, a mackerel sky speeded up, moving swiftly into a thick bank that soon blocked out every bit of the light. Adrift in the deepest blackest night he'd ever known, Jude opened his mouth to protest, and then realised Fareed's steady pace hadn't faltered. A soft beam of light shone out over the horse's head, showing just enough of the highway ahead, but look as he might Jude couldn't find its source. Focusing on that beam calmed him. The harder he tried to stay alert the more he started to doze.

"It hasn't stopped them," whispered Kid, snapping him back into wakefulness. "They have their own light. Look."

"Fareed can go faster than this." Jude raised the switch.

Tyrod stayed his hand. "We can't outrun them. It would be foolish to exhaust the horse with such a long journey ahead of us. Might as well stop and finish this now as later."

"Are you mad?" squealed Kid.

"So it has been said." Tyrod laughed. He stood and Fareed stopped so abruptly that Jude and Kid were thrown forward. In that same moment the clouds dispersed and bright moonlight illuminated the road. On their left, a thick oak wood lapped at the black highway.

"In amongst the trees," hissed Jude. "The longer he holds them off, the better chance we'll have." Jumping down they fought their way through thick brambles that tore indiscriminately at clothes and skin. The roar of the rust wreck was almost upon them now. Brambles gave way to shrubs and Kid went down on his knees and began crawling, tunnelling frantically into the depths of the wood, but Jude stopped to look back. Tyrod was standing in the middle of the highway, much as he'd stood waiting for the wagon. A small rust wreck came hurtling out of the darkness, searching the road with its one yellow eye and bearing all four of the meat-men on its back – two sitting astride, the others clinging precariously to its sides. Tyrod raised his staff; the rust wreck slowed and toppled over, still growling, wheels spinning, as its riders leapt clear.

"Turn back! Turn back! There is nothing for you here. The youngster is in my care now." His voice was, as his laugh had been, a thunderous boom, but this seemed closer, deafeningly loud, and it echoed along the valleys. All four meat-men hesitated. Then No-ears answered with a wordless roar and waved the rest on. A chorus of savage cries followed. They charged. Jude winced. He wanted to turn away, he wanted to run, to hide, but his eyes were locked on Tyrod as he waited, unmoving – except for his left hand, which almost imperceptibly drew open his coat. One minute he was beset by four attackers wielding sticks and knives and chains, the next, a flash of lightning and there was nothing more in front of him than four pillars of ash that the wind was already picking up and tossing into the air. Tyrod turned a little, and Jude caught a glimpse of something else that made no sense at all: inside the coat, where there should have been body, there were swirling galaxies, suns, moons, planets. He blinked and the impossible was gone. Like those earlier visions, it had probably never been. And yet …

"Kid!" Jude yelled. "Kid! Come back. It's all right. They're finished. Dead. Gone." He scrambled back towards the highway and examined its surface. A large area of crust had melted, he could feel the heat, but nothing remained of the men save a smooth black mark and a quantity of grey powder that the wind was now desultorily moving backwards and forwards. Jude looked at Tyrod. "What …?" he began.

Tyrod only pulled his coat more tightly round his chest. "Not yet, boy. Not yet awhile." The huge black birds flapped heavily to the ground, examined the powder and commenced a loud kronk-kronking that was all complaint.

"What's up with them?"

"No eyes to pick," said Tyrod, regretfully. "Doom and Destruction regard eye-balls as an after-battle delicacy."

# 3

Jude didn't mean to sleep – he needed to keep a close watch on this stranger. True, Tyrod made short work of their enemies, but that could simply be because he'd even more hideous plans for them. And yet sleep came, deep and sound and healing, untroubled by grief or fearful images.

When he woke it was dawn, a brilliant yellow-white dawn, and Fareed was out of harness, nipping grass on the banks of a river so wide that at first Jude couldn't see the far side. His eyes were dazzled by the sky's reflection – the water gliding past like liquid gold – but, growing accustomed to the glare, Jude made out a massive building beyond. Although its walls were not yellow as Oskar had far-seen, more nearly the ashen-cream of spoilt straw, Jude was convinced this was the one the dying man had spoken of, four spires like pointing fingers atop a great tower and many more spires below, rearing up as though from the river itself and silhouetted against an increasingly apricot-streaked sky. Tyrod stood facing the rising sphere, his coat held wide open. The grim black birds hunched one on each shoulder. Hearing Jude move they swivelled their heads completely round, regarded him silently, looked away. Jude showed his teeth to their backs. He patted the old horse's neck, noting to his surprise that no trace of yesterday's wound remained and moreover that there was a new sheen to his coat: it gleamed, almost copper, in the growing light.

Kid must have slipped from the seat some time in the night. Head on Ma's precious hand-fasting quilt, he lay amongst the spilled wheat, curled into a tight ball, hands clenched into tighter fists. The rope marks on his wrists stood out red and raw. The boy twitched in his sleep and, where the over-large jacket fell away, Jude saw teeth marks and a necklace of purple-yellow bruises flowering beneath the grime, but then his eyes slid down to the careful stitching of squares, oblongs and make-piece triangles that made up his mother's much-patched treasure. A lump rose in his throat at the thought of the many hours she'd spent, straining her eyes by fire light to preserve it, her daytime bawl and bluster temporarily gentled by the memories contained in every seam and fold. Loneliness descended, soaking into his soul, as cold and grey and relentless as November rain.

"Hey!" boomed Tyrod, striding up from the river. "We'll have no long faces here. It's too late for misery and too soon for guilt. Or is it the other way round? No matter. I'm hungry, boy. What about you?"

Jude shrugged. "We got some wheat. There are a few roots. And an apple or two."

"Is that so?" Tyrod snorted. The huge black birds glared. Jude, hastily making the secret sign to ward off sickness, saw that one had blue eyes, the other scarlet. Each lowered its head and stretched out its neck, uttering a series of loud kronks before taking off and flapping unhurriedly towards the heart of the sun. Kid came awake with a start, up on his feet in a single movement, fists still clenched and held before him. Seeing no threat, he emerged scratching and yawning.

"What was that?"

"Bluddy birds," muttered Jude, and relishing a forbidden word, used it again. "Pass us the bluddy wheat sack."

"Wheat! Grass heads are for dirt-grubbers and slaves, not warriors and destiny-makers." Tyrod gestured to half a dozen large fish-with-no-fins squirming and bucking on the grass. Taking a knife from one of his capacious pockets, he lopped off their heads, gutted the long bodies and flung the gubbins back towards the water. "Gather some wood, boy, and get a good fire going. I've a wolf in my gut. Maybe we'll need more of these." He strode back towards the river's edge.

There were few trees here. When Kid made off in the direction of a clump of willow, Jude padded after him.

"What you following me for?" Kid snarled.

Jude stared. "Getting branches for a fire."

"Find your bluddy branches somewhere else. I'm going for a pee."

"That's all right. I don't mind." He'd held regular peeing competitions with Tattow. Since Kid was so much smaller there was a better chance of winning today.

"Bluddy no!" yelled Kid.

Jude opened his mouth to yell back at the ungrateful squab who'd already forgotten being rescued but, remembering those glimpses of horribly battered body, swallowed his anger and turned away. He shuddered. Maybe there was more wrong with Kid than met the eye. Maybe he was really damaged. After a brief search Jude came across a cache of dry twigs. Taking off his jacket, he formed it into a sack, took a few fallen ash limbs under each arm and struggled back towards their campsite.

The eastern sky was streaked with red now. Not a good sign: red sky in the morning, traveller's warning. Jude kept his eyes down. He wouldn't, he really would not, look to the west with its domed bank of motionless cloud.

It was still there. He shuddered.

"I was told we must turn south by that tower," he said to Tyrod as they skewered the fish and hung them over the flames. Jude hadn't eaten flesh in a long time. His mouth began to water.

"South, that's right." Tyrod cleaned his hands on the grass. "Towards the summer lands, that's where we must go."

"But how are we going to get across the river?" There was no sign of either bridge or ford.

"Unless you want to swim, boy, we'll have to wait until she comes." There was reverence in Tyrod's voice. Jude wriggled as a frisson of excitement snaked up his spine.

"She? Who's she?"

"You know perfectly well of whom I speak." Tyrod turned to Kid. "And you've seen her too, I'm sure?"

"The lady?" Kid looked up from poking twigs into the fire. "Oh, yes. She's very pretty. How long will she be?"

"That I can't tell you; only a fool would attempt such prophecy. She'll come when she's ready. She must be here when the time is right. And the time is right when she's ready."

"Tyrod," Jude shuffled nearer, "tell me about my task."

"Hoo hoo!" boomed Tyrod. "Your task? *The* task, you mean. We're going to save the world, boy. We're going to save your world." He continued laughing to himself long after it had stopped being questionably funny.

"Yeh. Right. Ha ha. But what is it really?" persisted Jude – and shrank back as Tyrod's whole demeanour changed. The big man's expression became menacing. His body seemed to swell until it had doubled in size.

"Listen well, boy," he bellowed. "Creatures of the earth die, kinsfolk die, you, yourself, shall likewise die, but I shall never die, for I am the ruler of the skies, I am the summoner of souls and the bringer of victory. Do not presume to question my word, insolent whelp. Creatures of the earth die, kinsfolk die …" Tyrod's voice tailed away. He looked confused, shook his head as if to clear it, and muttered: "She will come soon. The time is almost right."

Full moon madness, thought Jude, remembering Bett, her self-important prophecies and her visions. Most of it had been nonsense. It would pass. Damned if he'd ask again though. He scanned the countryside, eager for a first glimpse of the woman.

All day they waited. Once again, the expected storm came to nothing. Jude and Kid gathered more wood. They collected flat stones and played ducks and drakes but – although Jude repeatedly tried asking about the other boy's past life – spoke of little that wasn't immediate. Tyrod lay near the wagon, arms behind his head and with the shapeless grey hat over his face. Hearing him snore, Jude crept closer thinking to twitch open the great coat and catch another glimpse of whatever it was he'd seen. He bent over, hardly breathing, one hand extended.

"Not if you value your sight, boy," said Tyrod, without moving. His blind eye was open and staring. Jude retreated, whistling his unconcern. He took a couple of sacks from the wagon and tossed one to Kid.

"We might as well look for foodstuff as lie around doing nothing like some people. You coming?"

"Long as you show me what I'm supposed to pick up."

"Anything we can eat, of course." Jude dealt him a supercilious sneer. "That your idea of a joke?"

"No. Only I ain't never been out in the wilds before. Not like this, anyway."

"Where d'you used to live then? On a cloud? In a cave? Bottom of a pond? *Under a stone?*"

"City," retorted Kid.

"Yah, get on. This ain't the old days. Nobody lives in cities."

"Shows how much you know," snapped Kid. "Loads of people do."

"Yeh? Yeh? Where then?"

"Somewhere else," Kid said, vaguely. He gestured towards the north. "It was somewhere colder with black stone walls everywhere. Dark skies, and always raining. I don't know how to get back. Bluddy don't want to, neither. "

"Loads of people?" sneered Jude, annoyed by his own wavering disbelief. "Next thing you'll be telling me is there are loads of *childs*, and all."

Kid nodded. "Yeh, a few. They was always locked up though." His chin went up. "I'm the only one what ever escaped – not that it was any bluddy better on the outside." His face suddenly looked more pinched than ever, and somehow greyer. "So if you want me to find food, show me what's what and where to look. I know what wheat's like and I've seen your apples, but mostly we just ate meat."

"What sort of meat?" Jude stared at him, wanting and yet not wanting an answer. His suspicions were confirmed by the expression on Kid's face before he shrugged and looked away.

"Any sort."

They were in luck: the pipberries, facing the sun, were dry and past eating here, but there were plenty of thorn-fruits, some witchberries, and beneath a dense old hedgerow, a mass of fallen cobnuts. It was Kid who discovered the apples on the far side, all sorts of apples, not wizened crabs these, but huge juicy orbs, golden yellow or flushed pink, green with red cheeks, orange mottled with crimson and rust. He also found the holes, hundreds of them, spread in an apparently random pattern between some ancient trees.

"Come here. Look." Kid dropped an apple core into one. "What's made that? Have to be a big rat. And it's really deep." He jumped back. Jude saw that here, too, the edges were peculiarly fuzzy and ill-defined; in flux. Many of the nearest holes seemed to be in the process of joining into larger ones. It was as if this land too was melting away, or rotting, at any rate ceasing to be.

Jude pulled at his arm. "Leave it. Let's go."

He hesitated, noticing that the holes seemed to radiate from the most ancient and mossiest tree of all, knobbled and bent and broken, loaded with clumps of mistletoe and bearing – as far as he could see – only one fruit. As he watched, it dropped into a tussock of rough grass and some instinct propelled him forward, picking his way between the holes, to snatch it up. Holding it by the stalk, Jude twirled it between his fingers. This was a perfect apple, the most beautiful he'd ever seen, red one side and bright gold the other, its unblemished peel taut and smooth and glossy. Tempted to bite into it straight away, he decided to save it for later and tucked it into a pocket. Old habits died hard and he took a small bunch of mistletoe almost without thinking. Ma and Bett would have stripped every branch.

As they made their way back to the riverside, bent under the weight of full sacks, Jude found himself looking more carefully at the ground. Now he saw that there were holes everywhere, most very small indeed, the largest no bigger than his little finger would fit comfortably into. He began to suspect that the entire landscape here was pitted with symptoms of this earth pox. Turning south would be a good idea and the sooner the better.

Tyrod hadn't moved, and Fareed was still grazing.

To Jude's surprise, two rabbits were peacefully nibbling the grass near the horse's head. He considered catching them – the fish-without-fins had been good and satisfying, whetting his appetite for more and it was a long time since he'd eaten proper meat – but the rabbits didn't move when he approached them, they showed no fear at all and, that being the case, Jude could not bring himself to club them, especially as such an act of violence was something he'd only seen from afar and never been called on to carry out himself.

Later in the afternoon, a pair of something else joined them: sleek, low slung animals, maybe the length of his forearm, reddish-brown above, stark white below, small-headed, sharp-featured, and with a long tail tipped black. Stoats, he thought, remembering also Tattow's minute description of their method of killing. He watched for a while, waiting for the zig-zag run, the pounce, the single death-bite at the back of the neck. But the stoats showed no inclination to attack. Instead they curled into sleep behind a wagon shaft.

"It's beginning then," commented Tyron, stretching so tall that his fingers seemed to scrape at the sky. "Ah, won't be long now. Doom and Destruction should be back shortly. Maybe they'll have some news."

"What's beginning?" asked Kid. "What won't be long?"

"Soon enough," said Tyrod. "Yes, all in good time. By-and-by. And if that's the way of it, we'd better eat while we can – nothing that's been summoned though. Have to be careful now. Things have changed. Shove some more wood on that fire, boy, let's have us a proper blaze."

"How will you know if something's *summoned*?" asked Jude.

"Have you ever seen the lamb and the lion lying down together before, boy?"

"The what?"

Tyrod snorted. "You'll know."

"What about your birds? Won't they kill the rabbits?"

"The law is the law, boy, even for ravens. Even for my ravens. No need anyway. There are always battles a-plenty at the end. Doom and Destruction will have flown far and fed well today."

Eyeballs, thought Jude, and wished he hadn't asked.

Evening came and sunset turned the river to blood. Tyrod brought yet more of the fish-without-fins from its crimson waters. The boys gathered a great pile of wood and stoked the fire until it raged against the darkness. They played knuckle-stones by its light – using worn pebbles from the shallows – until Jude grew tired of losing.

And still they waited.

As darkness fell, the temperature plummeted and a light frost spangled the grass. Overhead, there were more stars than Jude ever remembered and he looked to the south, trying to pick out the constellations Da had taught him. He couldn't even find the great winged horse. He risked a quick look west. The dense cloud was still growing. Plenty of stars there, too, but again nothing seemed quite right. Tyrod sat in silence, continually scanning the skies and repaying Jude's efforts at conversation with terse monosyllables, sometimes just grunts. Kid was no better. After crunching noisily through upwards of a dozen apples he climbed into the back of the wagon, crawled under Ma's quilt and pretended to sleep.

"What d'you want?" he snarled when Jude followed.

"To sleep. What d'you think?"

"Not in here you bluddy don't. You managed out there on that seat all right last night."

"It's bluddy cold."

"There's a fire, isn't there? And plenty of stuff to wrap around yourself. Here – catch! And this! Now clear off."

"But it's my wagon," began Jude, outraged. Above his head, the black birds shuffled and danced and whet their beaks against the curved rim of the roof.

"Not any more it isn't. Didn't you hear *him* say things have changed?"

Jude resentfully returned to the fire. He viciously stabbed an apple straight through its heart and held it in the fire, watching it blister and blacken over the flames. A low sound that might have been a chuckle came from Tyrod's direction, but the big man was still staring at the heavens.

Wrapping himself in the blankets, Jude settled down to sleep, but lay awake for a long time, missing the familiar after-dark sounds of his previous life: Ma's stentorian snore and Bett's mumbled incantations, Tattow and Summer's muffled squeaks and giggles, even Osker's racking cough. Here it was unervingly quiet – Kid made no sound, neither did Tyrod, though several times in the night he was woken by the multitude of small noises issuing from underneath the wagon – rustlings and murmurings, scrapings and witterings – that increased as the hours crept by.

Each time he woke Jude remembered the same dream. He'd been standing beside a hideous old woman, looking out over a great forest and seeing from afar a conical green hill rising from a sea of mist. On the summit of the hill stood a slender tower surrounded by an almost circular rainbow. Below the tower was a cave, blacker than the blackest night, within which writhed two great winged serpents – one fresh-blood red and the other death-skin white – guarding something precious, but what it was he couldn't make out. In the dream, he started to walk. A pounding began deep in the ground beneath his feet, swelling out into the woods and wild lands, into every rock and stone, into each creature that swam or slithered, crawled, ran or flew, every tree and leaf and blade. The nearer he came to the hill, the louder it became. In his dream Jude recognised that the pounding had always been there, underpinning the fabric of what is, for this was Earth's heartbeat. And though night by day it grew steadily faster, that heartbeat was failing. Something was required of him: he knew and yet did not know what it could be. Still dreaming, knowing he was dreaming, knowing that he'd always been dreaming, Jude swallowed his terror and kept walking.

When he woke properly it was to soul-flight time, the matt grey darkness that precedes daybreak. It was bitterly cold. The fire was dead. Stretching out his hands, Jude felt each blade of grass stiff with rime. Every out-breath became a small cloud drifting on the still air. And quieter than ever: the only sound was the infinitely varied song of the river as it hurried joyfully towards oblivion in the great sea at the end of all land.

As he watched, the thinnest nail-biting of gold appeared on the eastern horizon and Tyrod sprang up, strode without a word to the water's edge and repeated yesterday's unfathomable ritual. The black birds – his *ravens* – were already circling, riding the air currents high above; now they dropped like stones, alighting one on each of Tyrod's shoulders. Soon the sky became stained with pinks and oranges, splashed with violent red and purple, birthing another fiery dawn. Mist coiled along the river's surface.

Jude was hungry. He supposed that Tyrod would catch more fish-without-fins when he'd finished doing whatever he was doing. Getting the fire going would be a good idea, but finding something to sustain him seemed a better one. Apples would have to do.

Still wearing his blankets, Jude shuffled to the wagon and reached for the sacks stowed beneath the seat. Instead of stingweed cloth, his hands closed on thick fur. With a yelp, he sprang backwards, falling on his backside as the folds of cloth tangled round his legs. A sharp musky smell drifted down. The light was growing stronger by the minute and now he could see a host of creatures, large and small, carnivores and herbivores, assembled round and underneath the wagon, many that he had no names for, all watching him fixedly. Two thin-muzzled heads peered down from their vantage points. Those he did recognise. Their jaws were open, pink tongues lolling; it looked for all the world as if these creatures were laughing at him. Kid's face appeared behind them, wearing a stupid smirk.

"Nice dress."

"Bluddy foxes!" Jude rose with what dignity he could muster, grabbed the apple sacks, found them full of nothing but holes, and stamped off in search of firewood.

Today the ravens did not leave, but breakfasted resignedly on the heads and guts Tyrod tossed onto the grass.

And Tyrod himself seemed ill at ease. He paced. He snatched food from the fire, crammed it into his mouth without sitting and bawled forbidden words when it burned him. A tic started to twitch the skin under his blind eye. "Eat your fill, you two, but eat quickly." And when every flake of flesh had been picked from the bones, he threw more wood over the fragile skeletons and made sure the residue was consumed by the heat.

"What's up?" asked Kid, watching as he blew on the flames.

"Nothing," growled Tyrod. "Only that she doesn't like to see one creature eating another and now isn't the time to upset her."

"And why have all those *things* gathered?"

"Not things, but living creatures gathered two by two." Tyrod gave him a stern look. "Where it can be done, as long as it can be done, that's the way of things at these times."

"Oh." Kid wandered away and squatted by the wagon.

Jude followed him. The canvas was torn in places and a few willow leaves had caught in the roof frame. He yanked them off before hunkering down by the smaller boy. "None of them are frightened," he observed. "Funny, because whenever we saw any of these creatures before, they always ran and hid." With good reason, of course, since Bett and Ma could find ways of cooking anything Tattow managed to hunt down or snare. "Now they're seeking us out. Why?"

A hedgehog trotted forward and sniffed at Kid's fingers. He caressed its soft under-fur. The little beast hesitated for only a moment before moving on. Other creatures began to emerge from the dim interior or the shadows beneath the chassis and stood blinking at the bright light. Kid looked thoughtful.

"Maybe it isn't us they want."

"Who then?"

Kid stood up. "Her."

And there she was, the woman, more beautiful than ever in a dress woven from the harvest, its cloth the colour of falling autumn leaves – rust, gold, red, wine, all blending into each other – and with fruits Jude also had no names for superimposed. She came closer, walking so lightly that her bare feet hardly seemed to touch the ground. Round her slender waist lay a belt of plaited straw woven through with black nightshade and there were more strings of scarlet, green and yellow nightshade berries at her wrist and throat. Her hair had lightened to the pale gold of ripened wheat and lay loose on her shoulders. She approached Tyrod and they circled each other in what amounted to a stately dance. Each took the other's hand. Not a word was spoken. Her eyes fell on the two boys. When she smiled at Jude, his whole body reacted to her nearness; he yearned to be touched, he longed to be kissed, and he stepped forward, waiting to be held as Ma had sometimes done, but the woman's gaze slipped past him and alighted on Kid. Sorrow clouded her eyes. And immediately she opened her arms. Kid made a tiny sound, hardly more than a sharp intake of breath and ran to her. Jude watched sourly as the other boy stood pressed against her breast. The golden purr of pleasure dwindled and died.

Tyrod sighed. Jude sighed. He walked away and repeatedly kicked the far-side wheels of the wagon. A procession of other images danced over the surface of the canvas, faces that seemed familiar, brief glimpses of places that sparked a whole gamut of emotional responses. "No!" Jude hurriedly backed away. The sky shrank to a sliver of grey. Beneath his feet the parched grass turned fluid and set into solid stone; the wagon became a row of massed backs relentlessly pushing forward. "NO!" Jude struggled to hold on to reality – the tower, the river, the others – but their edges wavered and thinned until the wind carried them away. A hand caught at his arm as Jude turned to run.

"Wait! You can't go – everyone's relying on you to speak for us, for her."

Jude knew and yet did not know the voice, moreover he fought against remembering. "Too bad, I can't do it."

The small hand clung more tightly to his sleeve. "You *must*. You agreed. Someone's got to speak for her. Someone has to persuade them not to build over the last few acres of green."

"Not me," Jude screamed above the mounting din. "Better find some other mug."

The fingers dug into his arm. "It's your job. *You* took it on."

"Like hell I did. Nobody said it would be like this. You landed me with the job. What choice did I have? Leave me alone. Let go! fooking get off me! There's nothing we can do – too much money involved. Open your eyes. Can't you see we're walking into a trap? They're going to massacre us."

"Everyone has to die sometime."

"Not here. Not now." Tearing himself free, Jude fought against the tide of forward marching bodies. Then the great stream of water came, striking him full in the chest, hard as an iron fist, knocking him to the ground along with a whole swathe of other onlookers. Only it wasn't water. Flat on his back, he clawed at his stinging eyes, his burning skin. A roar of outrage rose above the howls and screams as those still standing surged forward. Eyes and nose streaming, Jude rolled over and struggled to his knees. His nose and ears were closing. Blisters numbed every exposed inch of skin. "Help me," he begged through thickened lips, but nobody answered. Above the turmoil, a voice too loud to be human bellowed orders to disperse; the crowd responded with an equally loud but wordless roar. A series of explosions ripped the air apart. Horses whinnied. More screams. En masse, the crowd turned and fled, trampling anything in its path. Jude found himself back on the ground, unable to breathe, face down in a puddle of the scalding liquid as feet pressed the remaining air from his lungs and crushed his limbs. A boot struck the side of his head and darkness reached out to enfold him.

Blinking rapidly, Jude lifted his face and saw coarse grass speckled with rabbit droppings. He was all right: his skin was undamaged; he could breathe, and hear. The square had melted, the crowd disappeared. But even as the terror drained from him, a sense of loss clutched at his heart, less immediate than the loss of his group, less raw than the grief he felt for Ma's absence, altogether deeper seated, a loneliness of the soul that was tinged with shame. It was only the sour after-taste of a bad dream, Jude decided, and thrust the feeling away. Nothing here had changed. Moreover, nobody had noticed him falling asleep on his feet.

"Come," said Tyron, bringing Fareed, "time to go south."

"And how we going to do that?" demanded Jude, trying to stare meaningfully at the river without looking at Kid and the woman, still standing close, still talking intensely, quite possibly exchanging tender caresses. "Fly?"

"Things will become clear, boy. Have patience."

"What's her name, anyway?"

Tyrod hesitated. "Unless she says otherwise, here you should call her Ersay."

"Oh." Jude fidgeted for a moment. "Tyrod, about this task of mine …"

"What of it?" Tyrod huffed with exasperation. "Come on, come on, boy. Spit it out. We haven't got all day. What's troubling you?" He peered intently at Jude. "I take it the nature of the task has been fully explained to you, such being the bounden duty of the travelling people? Self-indulgent and lazy though you've proved yourself, you're not totally ignorant?"

"No," snapped Jude, stung by the insult.

"So you understand the task?"

"Yes."

"All of it?"

"Everything," lied Jude.

"Good," said Tyrod, regarding Jude critically, "though a less likely hero I never saw. So what was your question?"

"Nothing. Doesn't matter."

"Very well." Tyrod backed Fareed between the shafts and gestured that Jude should see to the harness. "Now, boy, time to cross the river. Prepare for the journey."

"What?" Jude looked from Tyrod to the water and back again. "No, I ain't doing that. Poor old horse can't swim pulling the wagon. He'll drown. If you think I'm going to …"

"See to the harness!" thundered Tyrod, drawing himself to his full height and staring at him with the white eye. "And jump to it."

Jude jumped, muttering to himself all the while. He muttered some more when Ersay climbed into the wagon and Kid nestled against her. The small creatures silently swarmed up after them and disappeared into shadowed nooks and crannies at the back of the wagon. Jude tried to climb up, too, but Tyrod laid a firm hand on his arm.

"Lead the horse to the river's edge."

"Come on, Fareed." Jude's heart began to thump against his ribcage. He swallowed hard but did as he was told. As they approached the water it began to draw slowly apart so that a clear way two wagons or more wide appeared below, with the water gradually rearing up to a great height on either side. Jude tried not to think about impossibilities. Tyrod looked as if nothing out of the ordinary was happening – but what could you expect from someone who had a slice of the heavens tucked inside his coat? As for bluddy Kid, all he bluddy did was bluddy stare at Ersay.

Without waiting for more orders, Jude guided Fareed down the slope and on to the puddled track. At this level, the walls of water loomed even higher, and with infinitely more menace. Immediately, his feet sank deep into the soft mud. So did the wheels, creating such a drag that the horse tossed his head in alarm.

"Keep moving!" roared Tyrod, and pushed from behind.

The wagon lurched forward. Jude kept going, sick with terror, sensing the gathering force of the water pushing at invisible boundaries. If the river crashed back to its course, they'd all be drowned. Every outside sound was muted now; all he could hear was the mud sucking and glooping at his boots, the creak and graunch of the wheels. Spray rained down and soaked straight through to his skin making him flinch as he momentarily relived his dream. Several times the wagon sank up to the axles; each time Tyrod's mighty strength heaved it out again. Gibbering with fear, all Jude could do was look straight ahead, straining his eyes for a first glimpse of proper dry land, so that he didn't notice the chasm until it was almost too late. Fareed reared. He pawed at the air. He screamed. Tyrod started to push again and for a moment Jude and Fareed teetered on the precipice edge of a hole far bigger than the one in the red city. There was no water in the hole. No mud. Nothing.

"STOP BLUDDY PUSHING!" Jude took Fareed's head and backed him up a foot or two. Farther was impossible as the wagon's back wheels dug ever deeper into their own tracks.

"What is it, child?" asked Ersay, speaking to him for the first time. Her voice was sweet and low, beguiling as summer breeze through sap green leaves, welcome as a spring bubbling through ferns and cress at the side of a dusty track, but Jude thought of Kid and closed his heart.

"Hole," he said, briefly, "and there's no room to get round." He looked behind, gauging whether he could turn Fareed and get him back to where they'd started from. To his horror he saw the most distant walls of water gradually collapsing; already trickles of water were swirling into the deep ruts made by the wagon's wheels. Ersay's voice dispelled the churning panic.

"There, Jude," she said. "You may continue."

Where there had been hole, now there was – *something else* – something no less unreal. The new river bottom was nothing like the surrounding mud flat with its decomposing weeds and occasional flapping fish – for a start, the outline of the hole could still clearly be seen – but it had been overlaid with what looked like grey and gauzy net, grubby cobweb, a shadow of what once was. Jude was reminded of Bett's cobbled mending of old garments. He doubted it would take their weight. Tyrod ran at him, almost knocking him flat.

"Stop admiring the view, boy. Can't you see the water rising?"

To either side, the great walls of water far above his head were now curving precariously inwards. A fresh rush of water came from behind. And Tyrod was right: already it was lapping at his ankles. Without allowing himself space to think, Jude urged Fareed forward. There was a heart stopping moment of terror as they heaved their mud-weighted feet across the hole – for those few yards he couldn't see either the horse or the wagon, they simply ceased to be, and he dared not look at himself – then they had passed beyond it and a moment later were struggling up on to a marshy plain that was the river's opposite bank.

"Well done, boy!" boomed Tyrod, dealing him a mighty blow across the shoulders. But Ersay said nothing at all. Jude sneaked a quick look and saw her busy combing the tangles from bluddy Kid's bluddy hair. Not that he bluddy cared. No.

Behind them the waters met with a great roar; huge waves broke the surface, facing both up and down stream, slapping against the land, swirling in wild eddies, churning and frothing, and finally dying away as the river returned to its natural course. The lugs of the wheels were thickly clogged and mud was caked far up the sides. Angrily grabbing a handful of reeds, Jude scrubbed off as much as he could and was surprised to find fresh green leaves lodged in the wattle walls everywhere the canvas had split. This time they were more difficult to shift and, looking closer, he saw tiny green buds sprouting from almost every dead stick, both hazel and willow, woven into the basketwork that formed the walls and roof of the wagon. Tyrod seemed unconcerned.

"Everything is changing, boy. You'll understand by-and-by. All in good time. Wait and see." He stared towards the building with the spires and slapped Fareed's flank. "On we go then."

Jude led the horse along a high ridge running through the marsh. Small stones jutted from the grass here and he guessed they were travelling along an ancient causeway. Soon the marsh was behind them; narrow path grew into fairly wide track, and this in turn became a highway. There was no time for The Road Thing: Fareed sprang forward with such eagerness that Jude was forced into a run to keep up with him, but when he attempted to jump aboard the wagon, Tyrod hooked him back by the collar and usurped his place.

"No riding for you, boy. Exercise, that's what you need. Who ever heard of a hero with no waist?"

And Kid laughed. *Kid laughed.*

Mad with rage, Jude forced himself to keep abreast of Fareed as they finally turned south. He grew hot. His blood boiled. His wet clothes steamed. His nails dug into his palms and he bit down hard on his lip. In his mind Jude rehearsed terrible ends for the ungrateful, scrawny, bug-ridden turd that he, risking his own precious life, had taken the trouble to rescue.

Mid-afternoon the highway grew much wider and was joined by a twin, the two separated by a strip of tangled bushes. The going should have been easy now – much of the black crust being intact here – but Jude had never walked so far in his entire life, never mind run. His feet were raw and sore. He was exhausted, and still bitterly resentful. It wasn't right, three people riding in the wagon, anyway. Ma would never have stood for it, particularly when the three didn't include him. When the highway suddenly ceased to be, he sat down on the bank and found some sour-leaf to chew. Let somebody else work out what to do next.

"Such a thing wasn't supposed to happen." Tyrod descended from the wagon and peered into the great chasm that had eaten away both highways. "Time's running out."

"I can't be expected to remember everything," said Ersay, setting aside Kid to stand tall and beautiful on the ledge in front of the box. "Without their help at these times I can no longer always hold the picture of what is and was and will be."

On this occasion no effort was made to repair the hole. She looked down at Jude and smiled. His heart ached. He turned his face away.

"Half a day lost." Tyrod grunted. "No help for it. We'll have to turn back and find another way through."

"Someone else can do the walking then," said Jude, in the same moment noticing that the bank was pitted with small holes. He jumped up immediately, scowled, and sat down again. "Because I'm bluddy not."

Tyrod laughed. "You'll thank me for this spot of exercise soon enough."

"I bluddy won't!"

"On your feet, miserable whelp."

"No." Jude waited until the wagon was almost out of sight before trudging miserably after it.

They stopped for the night within sight again of the great building that Osker had far-seen. All the walking had been for nothing. Jude sprawled on the grass and watched Kid single-handedly haul back wood and set a fire. He narrowed his eyes at the long black hair freed from its tangles.

"At least it's easier for the bugs to run around now."

"You still sulking?" enquired Kid.

"Why would I be sulking?" scowled Jude. "What's there to sulk about?"

"Off your arse, boy!" thundered Tyrod. "Water the horse."

Grinding his teeth, Jude caught hold of Fareed and made for a streamlet running down towards the river. He punched the air and looked south towards the far hills. There was no reason for him to put up with this. It was his bluddy wagon. His bluddy horse. *His bluddy task.* The minute they turned their backs, he'd ditch the lot of them. As he took the horse's head again, Jude noticed the two ravens perched on a dead tree stump close by.

"Clear off!" he shouted, waving his arms.

Neither of the birds moved until he'd started trudging towards the camp site. Even so, they were back on Tyrod's shoulders long before Jude reached the wagon. To his disgust, Ersay was still fiddling with Kid's hair – getting the bugs out now, he supposed. Bett had herbal remedies for that sort of thing. Judging by what he'd seen, picking them out one by one would be a mighty long job. He'd be gone weeks before they were finished, so why should he care? Jude smiled to himself. Tyrod tugged at his beard and looked long and hard at him. He said nothing.

For a while, Jude sat apart, seething quietly and making his plans, but the night air grew so cold that it stung and soon he was forced to shuffle close to the fire. There would be a hard frost tonight. Besides, he was hungry.

"Aren't we going to eat?" He looked in vain for plump fish-with-no-fins.

"Indeed you are," said Ersay, and tipped from her skirt a magnificent selection of fruits, large and small, stone and berry, in every colour of high summer and autumn. At first, Jude ate reluctantly, then forgot his resentment as flavours he'd never known or imagined burst against his tongue. And the more he crammed into his mouth, the more appeared.

"What are their names?" he asked, wiping juice from his chin and hands. "Where do they grow?"

"You don't need to know their names," Tyrod said gruffly. "Each and every one of us, each and every thing, will need to take a new name at the journey's beginning. That's always been the way of it."

"Don't you mean journey's end?" asked Kid, puzzled.

He fixed the boy with his blind eye. "Is there a difference?"

"Yes."

"Not in a circle," said Tyrod. He held up his hand. "Enough. Now that all of us are gathered, there are things that must be spoken of. First, from now on there will be no stopping at night. We make all speed towards the place."

"There are many creatures that haven't answered the call yet," Ersay said, softly. "My doves … "

Tyrod frowned. "Yes, yes. There is still time. Even so, our journey should take less than three days and three nights."

"Unless there are any more holes," muttered Jude, glumly wondering how he would steal away if the wagon was in constant use.

"Indeed." Tyrod glanced at Ersay. He tugged at his beard. "Hmmm. Well. The second thing is this: all things have conspired to bring us together. There is no escaping this journey for either of you." He glared at Jude, who shrank back. "Do you hear me, boy? Good. However, when we get to the place each of you will be given the choice to carry out your appointed task, or not. Third …"

"Wait a minute," said Jude. "You mean Bug-head has a task too?" Ersay and Tyrod looked at each other and laughed.

"There is only one task." Tyrod laughed some more.

"Of course," said Ersay. "Why else would Kid be here?"

"Only because I rescued …" began Jude, but was interrupted by the clenched fist Kid shook under his nose.

"Stop calling me Bug-head, fat arse. Tell you what – the bugs will go. Colour of your hair won't."

"You want a thump?"

"Like to see you bluddy try, double-gut!"

Jude's knuckles glanced off Kid's nose. It surprised both of them. Kid recovered first.

"Fook you!" he bawled, pushing Jude hard in the chest. Jude staggered backwards, righted himself, and swung a punch at the other boy's head. Kid ducked, slippery quick, and kicked his ankle hard. "Yah, fat and slow," he jeered, dancing around Jude as he squealed and hopped, "too fat and slow to catch me!"

"Oh, yeh?" Jude suddenly lunged, caught an edge of Kid's jacket, hauled the boy in, and used the whole of his weight to knock him to the ground. He pummelled as much of Kid as he could reach. "And fook you, too!" he screamed, relishing the use of a forbidden word.

Tyrod pulled them apart. "This is no time for play."

"Play?" panted Jude, boiling with rage and flailing the air. "I ain't playing. Let go of me. I'll finish him off, see if I don't. I'll rip his guts out and stamp on them. I'll shove his balls down his throat. I'll … I'll … I'll tear his head off and stick it on top of the wagon to frighten off birds. Pity I rescued the stinking runt. Wish I'd left him where he was …"

Ersay's sweet low voice restored Jude to his senses.

"Stop now," she said, placing one beautiful hand on his shoulder. Jude slowly subsided and took a tiny step towards her, his eyes fixed on her breasts, losing himself in a hunger he didn't totally understand. He breathed in Ersay's fragrance, which seemed to be compounded of his favourite smells – wood strawberries and raspberries, yellow plums, jessnuts, honey – but it wasn't that sort of hunger. He wanted ... Jude blinked and lifted his eyes to her face, wishing for ... he knew not what ... perhaps simply that she would take him in her arms and kiss him. Ersay smiled and shook her head as if he'd asked aloud. She moved away. "I sent you to rescue Kid, Jude. Don't you remember me showing you the way?"

Jude nodded, struck dumb.

"Kid has suffered much." Ersay sighed. Jude reluctantly nodded again and glanced towards Kid, but he was standing hunch-shouldered and staring at the ground. "You, Jude, may yet suffer even more ..."

At her words a cold shiver ran down Jude's back. He was suddenly very afraid. Nobody had told him the task might be dangerous.

"What ..." he began, but again Ersay shook her head.

"And perhaps there will come a time when the favour has to be returned."

"*Him* rescue *me*?" The idea was so comical that Jude's previous terror at her words dissolved and left him snorting with laughter. Kid's eyes flashed. He bared his teeth and his fists came up. Tyrod intervened before either of them had the chance to recommence hurling insults and punches.

"ENOUGH. As I was saying, each of you will be given the choice to refuse the allotted task if cowardice gets the upper hand." He looked each of them up and down with his one good eye and smiled sardonically. "From what I've seen so far, this may yet end in disaster. I reserve judgement on that. Third ..." Tyrod tapped his middle finger, and again Jude saw that glint of silver. "Third, my ravens see all, hear all, and sense all. They are my gatherers of news. Even your most secret thoughts are not safe from them." He glared at Jude, who blushed and looked away. Then the huge man rose and clapped his hands together. "And now sleep well, for I guarantee tomorrow will surprise you with the scale of its changes."

# 4

All morning they travelled along narrow highways that twisted and turned – always climbing – and often disintegrated into the roughest of tracks. Large ruins gave way to small, heath land to scrub. Soon, thick woods pressed in on either side.

Today, Jude found the going easier. It was as if he'd tapped into some innate rhythm, previously unsuspected. He minded more now that the others were sitting than that he was walking. From time to time he looked back at them to see what was going on. Kid always noticed and slyly crossed his eyes, stuck out his tongue, or puffed out his cheeks, holding the slack of his jacket away from him as though to accommodate a huge stomach. Jude ignored him ... apart from drawing his thumb swiftly across his throat and miming the wringing of a scrawny neck. Even that stopped when Tyrod caught his eye. Ersay seemed to be enjoying the journey. Sometimes she sang while Tyrod marked time with his staff and the bug-head creature joined in with a shrill and silly voice that proved his balls hadn't dropped.

Three times they were forced to retrace their steps.

The first was where a crumbling wall of flat yellowish stones ran alongside a stand of mighty beech trees. As the wheels crunched across the mast, Jude thought of Ma painstakingly peeling sackfuls of the tiny nuts, crushing them to make butter; he remembered Bett stripping beech bark to cure her winter rheumatics. The ache of loss made his spirits sink just as the track dipped into a shallow coomb. And there the land ended. In the distance dark conifers seemed to float in mid air.

Ersay stood up and looked about her. "I have no memory of this place," she murmured, plaintively.

"Turn the wagon round, boy," said Tyrod. "Try another path."

It was not too much of a problem. There were tracks everywhere here, a giant spider's web of by-ways weaving in and out of the trees. Before long, taking their bearings on the sun – today a fuzzy disc in a foggy white sky – Fareed was heading south again. But the process was repeated as they made their way through forest so dense that little sunlight entered and where clumps of dank brown leaves fell on them like wet rags. Jude shuddered. This was an evil place that seemed to cast its own desolate shadow. There was something else, too: the clatter of Fareed's hooves was muffled by the thick mulch underfoot here and Jude picked up another sound, faint and far off, a noise from a nightmare that made his hair stand on end. He strained his ears, but the sound was not repeated and Jude finally dismissed it as a trick of the wind forcing its way through tight-packed branches. Then he forgot about it altogether, for without warning they came upon another absence of land.

This time proved far more dangerous: the chasm, a well of intense darkness in a place of ink black shadows, was hardly visible. There was no space to turn. The wagon had to be backed until an opening in the trees was reached. And when they tried working their way along a track running parallel, found themselves confronted by the chasm's outer perimeter and had to retreat again.

"I cannot ..." Ersay's voice tailed away. She shook her head.

Tyrod's face was grim. "We must hurry."

"We can't go any faster," retorted Jude. "Yeh, Fareed's slowed down, but he's been walking since daybreak. And so have I."

"Too bad." Tyrod brought his face so close that Jude couldn't avoid looking at the crinkled white eye, the veined and pitted nose with its maelstrom vibrissae. "Hurry. I mean it, boy. I said there'd be changes. Not all of them will be for the better."

Jude gritted his teeth and out of sheer spite started off again without waiting for Tyrod to regain his seat. There had indeed been changes. For all that he acted the same as usual Kid looked completely different this morning. His black hair shone. His brown skin glowed. Furthermore, not only had the bruises faded and some of the tension drained from his body, but Jude was sure the scrawny runt had grown an inch or two. Not that they'd spoken more than a few words, Kid's reticence was no less, and anyway, why speak when their mutual dislike could be conveyed in a few pertinent gestures? Jude's quick backward glance took in all three of the wagon's occupants. Yes, Bug-head had definitely grown, and filled out, too. Tyrod and Ersay, on the other hand, seemed – frailer wasn't quite the right word, nor weaker – but different too, and not in a good way.

He took Fareed's head and tried encouraging him to trot. The old horse did his willing best until he was defeated by the track's gradient. Soon it grew so steep that Jude demanded everyone climb down and push the wagon. Ersay did not, but a fierce look from Tyrod quashed any idea of insistence. Only when the crest of the hill was finally reached did Jude remember the extra load of small animals secreted in the back of the wagon. And of course the wagon itself must be heavier now that every cleft and stave had burst into leaf.

Jude guided Fareed onto a patch of grass. "He needs a rest. And a drink."

Tyrod said nothing. The ravens glared from his shoulders and a few feathers drifted to the ground. Jude grinned. Doom and Destruction were moulting. A featherless bird was a dead bird. Everyone knew that.

"Are you hungry?" asked Ersay, as he reached into the wagon for the water barrel. Jude nodded, though he couldn't have said whether it was hunger or greed. There had been further delicious fruits at breakfast, sweeter, too; the more he'd eaten, the more he wanted. Even now, his mouth watered at the thought. But this time he was disappointed: the fruits had lost their bloom; many were wrinkled, brown-speckled, desiccated. Jude caught Kid's eye. The other boy shrugged and carefully sorted through the pile until he'd found a satisfactory handful. Jude followed suit. Of these, some had a fousty back taste, others were sour and vinegary. He looked at Ersay, who was now anxiously scanning the distant hills, and saw that her dress had become browner and darker. In places, the hem was ragged. A few bright beads had fallen. The plaited belt was slowly disintegrating though the ink-black nightshade berries still clung. To his horror he observed faint wrinkles puckering the skin around her beautiful eyes and mouth, fine lines barring her forehead. He swallowed hard, fearing he knew not what. But then Ersay smiled full in his face and Jude's heart leaped just as it had that very first time on the way to the red city. And since she no longer fussed over Kid he allowed himself to return that smile. He would do anything for her, anything, lay down his life if necessary … Jude waited in vain for Ersay to open her arms to him, to kiss him as he'd seen her kiss Kid, but even as he basked in the warmth of her smile his vision skewed, the world turned grey and bleak, the grass solidified, howls and yells battered his eardrums, a hand tugged at his sleeve.

"It's your job. *You* took it on," insisted the eerily familiar voice.

Jude shook his head violently. "Like hell I did. Leave me alone! fook off!"

"What's that?" demanded Kid, through a mouthful of fruit.

"Can't you see we're walking into a trap? They're going to massacre us."

"Who is? Where? What's got into you?"

"Everyone has to die sometime," whispered the voice in his ear.

The scene changed abruptly. Now he stood in a forest clearing. Winter: bare trees clawing the sky with iron grey fingers, the ground speckled with recent hail stones, and yet it was not cold. Flames leaped at the periphery of Jude's vision; a red gold glow mellowed the squalid front of each hovel. His eyes burned from the pungent smoke. The air tasted greasy. The stench of burning flesh filled his nostrils. Rigid with fear and grief, he stared straight ahead, not daring to turn his eyes in the direction of the agonised screams.

"Speak out," urged the voice. "You *must*. You agreed. She did. Now someone's got to speak for her."

The screams grew louder, more agonised. Close by, a low whimpering began. Jude clenched his teeth and swallowed the sound. A sharp elbow in his ribs brought him back to reality.

"You asleep with your eyes open?" Kid jabbed him again. "Sounded like you was grizzling. Snap out of it, bluddy loony!"

"Leave off." Jude shuddered and ratcheted open his fists. A neat line of bloody crescents marked where his nails had dug too deep into his palms. Bad dream, that's all it was; yeh, day dream turned sour by the manky fruit, nothing more. He saw that Ersay and Tyrod had already returned to their perches on each side of the box, and the big man awarded him such a black look that Jude hurriedly reached for Fareed's rein. "Better get going."

But the echoes of those terrible cries stayed with him. Nothing would shift them. Jude put his head down, gritted his teeth and forced his feet to keep moving as he tried to overlay the images with pleasanter memories. So preoccupied was he, that it took a while to register that the sounds of a different nightmare had returned, louder this time, and nearer.

"You hear anything?" he demanded of Kid, who'd been loping alongside Fareed, throwing grains of wheat at the ravens who obliged by craning their necks and snapping each one from the air. "Listen. Now. Over there."

Kid bent his head and listened. "That? Yeh. So what? Next thing is you'll be frightened of your own fat shadow. Only the bluddy wind in the trees, ain't it?"

"No." Jude shook his head. It wasn't the wind. It never had been. "Look at Fareed." The horse's nostrils were flared, his ears back, and now he began dancing sideways, rolling his eyes as the noises became howls that steadily grew louder; closer.

"That's a fooking dog pack!" breathed Kid, grabbing a hefty stick.

"Or wolves," said Jude, peering into the darkness of the forest. He tried to hurry Fareed but the horse would not be hurried. Without daring to turn around, he yelled: "Tyrod, can you hear them?" His mouth was dry. His hands were shaking. Some of the most horrific of Tattow's stories had been of wolf packs prowling battlefields heaped high with the dead and dying, or hunting down stranded travellers. Jude tried to remember what the heroes of those tales had done to vanquish the wolves, but could only recall everything they'd had to contend with – giant dog-like creatures, as tall as him at the shoulder, maybe taller, with red eyes and scimitar claws and double rows of blade-sharp teeth. A full grown wolf, Tattow had assured him, could eat fifty men and then look round for more. They were almost invincible, too: cut them down and next morning they jumped up whole again.

The howls grew louder; closer. There was a long moment of eerie silence, followed by a great snapping and crashing of undergrowth. Kid screamed, dropped his stick and leaped for the wagon as fifteen maybe twenty lean bodies erupted from amongst the trees. Not wolves, but dogs, dogs of all shapes, sizes and colours, growling and snarling, barking and yelping, edging close enough for Jude to see their slavering mouths and huge pointed teeth – never mind that they only possessed one set apiece – and the vicious hate in their eyes. He laid about him with the switch, aiming for their noses.

The dogs retreated, but it was only temporary. And now Jude remembered Ma's stories of dogs maddened by shortage of water and surplus of blood. They never gave up. She'd sometimes used them to scare him into silence when he couldn't sleep. "Shh, or the blood dogs will come for you." Well, they'd come now. But it was clearly Fareed they wanted. A great yellow creature leaped snarling at the horse's throat. Fareed reared, pawing the air, and his hoof smashed the dog's skull. It fell, but three more took its place.

"Tyrod!" yelled Jude. One brief flick of a lapel and the dogs would be no more. "What's Tyrod bluddy doing? I can't hold them off for ever."

"He's not here," wailed Kid. "They've both gone."

"Fook!" Gone? Where – and when? It didn't make sense. Jude continued to lay about him, occasionally getting in a hefty kick for good measure, but it was clear that this was a fight neither he nor Fareed could win. The dogs showed no sign of tiring. There were too many of them, with more closing in from all directions. They were getting bolder, too, each time coming nearer and retreating for a shorter distance between lunges. A mean little dog streaked from the pack and began nipping at Jude's ankles, distracting him as another leapt for his switch arm, its teeth tearing through the cloth to puncture the skin. "TYROD!" Drawing back his other fist, Jude punched the dog until it loosed its hold and tumbled under Fareed's great feathered hooves. With its yelps still ringing in his ears, he lifted the smaller dog up on his boot and kicked it into the trees. Dripping sweat, Jude turned to face yet another attack.

And then it was over. The snapping and snarling ceased abruptly. The dogs fell back. A few whimpered. Some lay down, noses between their forepaws, others slunk off, tails tucked under, into the gloom of the forest. Jude didn't need telling that Ersay and Tyrod had returned. He ran at the wagon, narrow-eyed with rage.

"Where were you? We could have been killed. And Fareed ..."

"Do you dare to question us, boy?" roared Tyrod. "What's all the fuss about? I see no injuries. You're still on your feet."

"No thanks to you," retorted Jude.

Ersay silenced him with a gentle touch. "Jude, understand that we have other endings to oversee, other beginnings to protect. You are not the only beings occupying this place. Others walk beside you, unseen. Others live in the spaces between one moment and the next. Yet others inhabit the spaces inside the spaces."

"Oh," said Jude. He gave Kid a sidelong look, wondering if this had made any sense to him. "Get that?"

Kid spread his hands and hunched his shoulders. "Clear as mud."

"Never mind," Ersay smiled. "What's important is that you are unhurt and that I found my doves."

Jude jumped back as she took two pure white birds from her bodice. The paler the bird, the worse the sickness; everyone knew that. And white birds were the worst of all, white being the colour of death. The filthy things fluttered down onto Fareed's collar, spreading their fan-shaped tails and making subdued cooing noises deep in their throats.

"Get away from me." Jude waved his arms and the doves flew up to perch on the curved rim of the wagon's roof. The ravens eyed them balefully. When Jude remembered to look again the doves had disappeared. He grinned to himself. With any luck the ravens had swallowed them whole.

Somewhere between that stop and the next, the wagon began to flower with a false spring and by mid-afternoon was hung all over with the tasselled catkins and tiny red sunbursts of hazel, and the fat yellow rabbit tails of the willow. A few sprays of wild cherry blossom appeared, a cluster of dog roses. Tendrils of honeysuckle twined around the chain that ran between the shafts, and no matter how many times Jude ripped it off, when he looked again it had grown back, stronger each time, more persistent, occasionally even reaching forward to nose at Fareed's great feathered feet. Perhaps, Jude thought, it was the unseasonable flowers that brought the insects. They came in a vast cloud that swallowed the light; the very air sang with their presence. Afterwards, the silence baffled the eardrums and there was a sense of emptiness. Then the birds arrived, led by a pair of corpsepeckers, descending on the wagon in a continuous rain of multi-coloured bodies, so many, and so loud, that the disgruntled ravens took off to flap, tree to tree, alongside.

Jude shrank from the birds. Why would Ersay want them? And especially the corpsepeckers, the harbingers of evil. He beat at the air with the switch. He muttered aloud the charms and mantras learned at Ma's knee, and soon all was quiet again save for Ersay's murmurings, Tyrod's occasional growl, and the wind keening as it tried to strip whole forests of their leaves.

As he walked, Jude kicked at the spiny cases of false jesssnuts until the glossy brown seeds erupted. From long habit he snatched up a red and white-spotted bug-agaric, stuffing it deep into a pocket before remembering with a fresh pang of grief, that there would be no more trading with Tattow for honeycomb or a finely whittled pipe.

From time to time, a vision of that other forest intruded on his consciousness, complete with stench and screams and choking smoke. The fear receded but the grief lingered, and another faint guilt began to grow in him, for a sin of omission, a base act of betrayal that teased and taunted on the tip-of-tongue-edge of memory.

On they plodded. The light was beginning to change when they reached a headland overlooking what must have long ago been an inhabited valley – perhaps even a small city – judging by the ruins round the circumference of the largest hole in the land yet. These were the remains of fine substantial buildings, made of stone blocks. From this distance several appeared sound, with intact roofs, doors, even, here and there, the glint of window glass. Jude tried to imagine the old days, where settlements such as this swarmed with life. His eyes were drawn to a few dark figures scrambling up a steep slope on the far side. Like a living thing, the hole stealthily chewed away the ground behind them. As Jude watched mesmerised, a whole line of walls was simply blotted out, then the trees behind it, part of the slope, a ...

Tyrod clouted him so hard that Jude reeled from the blow. "Turn back, fool! Turn back!"

Jude obeyed quickly enough. He led the weary horse back along the short stretch of highway and onto a narrow track running at right-angles to it. The setting sun was still little more than a brighter patch in the matt white sky. Keeping it on their right he twisted this way and that along tracks and by-ways through a network of valleys until they were once again heading south on a decent stretch of highway with the dying settlement behind them.

When the hand grabbed at his sleeve, Jude flinched and kept walking, concentrating with all his might on putting one foot in front of the other in a determined effort to keep his mind free of whatever guilts and miseries more visions might bring. But it was Kid.

"We ain't alone," he breathed. "There's bluddy five or six of them been following us since we turned off the tracks."

"Tyrod still here?"

"Yeh, but …"

"Tell him, then. He'll soon get rid of them." And, Jude thought, this might be the perfect opportunity to see what really lay under the old man's coat.

Kid sneered. "You really think I'd be talking to you if I could wake him? They're both flat out inside – fast asleep and snoring."

"Better try a bit bluddy harder," advised Jude, mentally rehearsing punching the other boy hard in the mouth, "because we've got precious little to defend ourselves with." Tattow had maintained what weapons he could – notably an unpleasantly sharp double axe, but it wasn't in the wagon – since he'd carried them with him most of the time, these had probably all been lost in the red city. Jude let his eyes slide sideways. Kid was right, and worse: not only were dark shapes moving purposefully through the trees on both flanks, but two more were in front, battling out of the undergrowth intent on blocking the highway ahead. Jude moistened his lips. He reached for the switch and stooped to pick up a large stone. Fareed whinnied and stopped as the two men emerged from the bushes and began swaggering along the highway towards them. Jude took one look and slunk back to stand against the wagon. Not only was he was still drained from battling it out with the dogs, but these were large men, even tougher-looking than Tattow and with nothing left to lose. Besides, both brandished unsheathed knives. Unless Tyrod intervened, they didn't stand a chance.

Behind him, Kid continued to bawl and shout in Tyrod's ear. By now the men were within a few paces of the wagon. Kid fell silent. The skulkers in the bushes had also closed in. Jude attempted to calm himself as he took their measure: two more men, one slightly built, mean-faced and squint-eyed, the other fat and greasy, his skimpy tunic revealing a waterfall of bellies hanging in folds over ragged trousers. These, he thought, presented less of a threat – although they clutched stout sticks both kept their eyes on the more pugnacious pair with the knives. There were also two women: one tall, straw-haired and cadaverous, the other as wide as she was high and with a fixed smile full of such menace that a scowl would have been infinitely preferable. So far, both women were hanging back but, remembering Ma's ferocity when crossed, Jude didn't discount them.

A wave of relief washed over Jude as he felt someone step onto the box behind him. But it was not Tyrod. It was Ersay. His spirits sank. Maddened dogs were one thing, would-be slavers another.

"Nice," said the first man, taking hold of Fareed's mane. He sheathed his knife. "Very nice – a bonus, I'd say. Step out of the way, boy. Your Ma and us won't be needing your services from here on."

"Fook off," snarled Jude deepening his voice to something he hoped approached Tattow's. He raised the stone. "And you can take your filthy paws of that horse."

"I can. I will. But not yet." The man grinned, showing stumps of dark brown teeth. His breath stank of old meat and his jacket hung open revealing body hair as thick and black as Da's hunting dog that had run alongside the wagon long seasons ago. He nodded at Ersay who remained silent and motionless. "I dare say I'll have other uses for my paws shortly."

Jude flung the stone, but his hands were shaking so much that he missed. His fingers tightened on the switch. "Touch her and you'll regret it," he said, fighting to keep his voice from trembling.

Stump-teeth threw back his head and laughed. The others joined in. From the corner of his eye, Jude saw the women moving closer. Straw-hair began fiddling with the canvas.

"Get out of there!" Jude bellowed. "I'm warning you ..."

Stump-teeth slapped his thighs, overcome by mirth. "Hear that, Si? The fat boy's warning us!"

"Is that so?" Si stepped forward, bringing with him a smell of putrescence that could only have come from the badly tanned hides wrapped round his frame and stitched into a rough approximation of garments. "What you going to do, fat boy?" He peered up at Ersay, glanced questioningly at Stump-teeth. "Bit of an old cow for what you've got in mind, ain't her?"

"Beggars can't be choosers. Many a good tune played on a very ancient fiddle, so they say, especially if you ain't got many choices." Stump-teeth waited for the others to finish sniggering and then made as if to climb onto the wagon. "We'll soon see."

"No!" Jude lashed out with the switch, catching him across the side of the face. Stump-teeth raised his hand to his cheek. His eyes widened as he brought back fingers covered with blood. At the sight of the blood the man of many bellies whimpered and turned away.

Straw-hair let out a yelp as some creature inside the wagon nipped at her prying hands. "They got meat in here," she announced, licking her thin lips. "Live meat. Fresh."

Stump-teeth silenced her with an imperious gesture. "Oh, you done it now, fat boy. You really have gone and done it. There was me being all nice and friendly and you go and spoil my good looks just when I'm going to get it on with your old Ma here." He suddenly lunged forward and snatched the switch from Jude's hand, at the same time punching him hard in the stomach. Jude doubled over, retching, gritting his teeth in his determination not to cry out. Stump-teeth laughed again. "What shall we do with this one, Si? You want him, ladies? You got any inclinations in that direction?"

"Might have," said the rotund one, rolling her eyes, "might have. I could do with someone to bite my toe nails short and scrape my back clean. Fires ain't all out yet neither."

"Dirty bitch," announced Squint-eyes.

"Sticks and stones," said she. "Perhaps you're that way inclined. Is that the trouble? Speak up, I ain't averse to sharing. On the other hand, plenty of meat on him, ain't there?"

"Go fook yourself," advised Jude. "See what happens if you put so much as a finger near either of us."

Stump-teeth sniggered. Straw-hair sidled closer.

"Let me play with him," she begged, nursing her hand. "There ain't much left to do of an evening. I can peel him and make a nice coat. I can read what the future holds from his spilled guts. And when I've finished, I'll lower what's left into one of them there holes bit at a time and see what happens."

"Very good," said Stump-teeth, approvingly, "but first I'm going to let him watch the proceedings with his Ma, if you see what I mean. After that, you two can fight it out over who's having him and for what ... No, wait," he held up the blood-stained hand,

"and then, we cut the meat off him, and *then* you can push him down one of they holes. Only thing is, I'll probably die pissing myself laughing. Now, where was I? Ah, yes …" Stump-teeth stopped suddenly in the act of heaving himself onto the box. He twitched and looked down. His eyes widened. "What the fook …"

He clutched at his genitals. A puddle was gathering round his boots, growing wider and wider, impossibly wide, filling the ruts in the highway with steaming liquid, running in streams and rivulets beneath the wagon and beyond. At the same time, beads of sweat sprang from every inch of exposed skin. The beads became a falling sheen of liquid slicking his chest hair. Water poured from every orifice: his nose ran; tears oozed from his eyes, joining forces with the copious saliva bubbling over his chin. His clothes began to steam. Si ran several paces, before turning to watch, his eyes wide with horror. Jude's own eyes felt as though they would start from his head because Stump-teeth was visibly shrinking, drying up, retreating into himself like a pond in the fierce heat of summer, his skin wrinkling like ungathered plums at first frost. Within minutes, Stump-teeth was half the man he'd been – and still shrinking. Finally, he collapsed into a patch of stingweed and lay kicking and thrashing. Fareed fidgeted, shying away from his shrieks of terror.

"Now laugh," said Ersay.

Jude glanced at her face and felt an additional chill run up his spine. Ersay might have been wearing a mask, so stern and pitiless was her expression, so hard her eyes, so cruel and set her beautiful mouth. Now he understood why she welcomed the corpsepeckers.

"Fooking witch!" howled Si, bounding back towards the wagon. Then he too, stopped dead and looked at himself in surprise as the skins tied around him began to flex and ripple and rejoin. A horn erupted from one shoulder, another from his breastbone. A large tongue lolled from his chest and two cloven hooves sprouted from a thigh. A pale udder forced its way through the hide draped across his stomach. "No!" Si started to scream and plead as his head was forced to one side by the rapid growth of a large wet nose beneath his Adam's apple. "Stop! Please. Have mercy. I wasn't going to do nothing. It was a joke."

"*That* is an old cow," said Ersay.

"I didn't mean none of it!" screamed Straw-hair, diving back into the undergrowth with the others. "It was all his idea."

"Drive on," commanded Ersay.

Jude didn't need telling twice. He snatched up the switch with trembling hands and persuaded Fareed into something approaching a canter. Behind them, Si's howls deepened towards bass and died abruptly. The horse slowed to his usual stoical plod and soon the only sounds were the familiar ones of hooves against the highway and the creaks and groans of the wagon.

"I'm sorry," Jude mumbled, looking back at Ersay. "I'm really sorry that I couldn't …" He felt ashamed that he'd been incapable of protecting her.

"For once you spoke up for me," she said, and smiled. "No matter that you were unable to defeat them alone. You took a stand. That was enough. It is a start."

"Fook," muttered Kid, emerging from his hiding place. "She sorted them out good and proper."

"No thanks to you," snapped Jude, still puzzling over Ersay's words. "That's the bluddy second time you didn't even try to help."

"And you did what exactly?" enquired Kid. "They was really frightened of you, I don't fink."

"At least I didn't run away and hide. *Twice.*"

"Bit difficult," smirked Kid, "with a gut like yours."

Jude bared his teeth. "Just wait."

"Ooh, I'm so scared."

"You won't have time to be scared, stinking little runt."

"Fatty."

"Scrawny coward."

"No more," said Ersay. "I told Kid to remain hidden, and with good reason. We will speak of this no more. Agreed?" She waited until both boys unwillingly assented. "Just remember that the punishment will always fit the crime."

Jude gave her a sidelong look. What was that supposed to mean? There was a long silence.

"You all right?" asked Kid, finally, observing Jude massaging his bruised stomach.

"Nothing wrong with me," Jude grunted.

"He didn't half punch you one. If you're hurt bad, I can take over."

"As if you care, you bug-headed turd. Piss off and hide."

Kid sniggered. "At least you ain't blubbing. That makes a nice change."

"You will be, soon as I get you on your own."

"Ah," said Tyrod, emerging from his slumber with a snort and a gulp. "Had a bit of a scrap? Why didn't you wake me? I could have done with the exercise."

"You want exercise then try walking for a change," muttered Jude, hastily moving out of range of Tyrod's staff arm.

The old man surveyed him with a sardonic eye. "As I said before, who ever heard of a hero with no waist? No waist and a fat behind, to make matters worse. You think to represent me in that state? Keep walking, boy. Keep walking."

At least this time Kid didn't laugh. Or if he did, it was surreptitiously. Just as well, raged Jude, or the bluddy flea bite would have no bluddy teeth left after he was bluddy called to bluddy account.

They began to climb again. Twilight thickened round them as the hours slipped by. The shadows deepened.

At that point where the world lay poised between day and night, when colour was leached from the woods and open spaces leaving everything sooty grey, fuzz-edged, but not yet black, Ersay stood up on the box and began to sing. Or rather, singing was the only way Jude could describe the sound which was high-pitched, rising and falling in ways which should have been pleasant but somehow set the teeth on edge and the back of his neck prickling. It wasn't just him that found the tunes uncomfortable listening. Above Ersay's head, the ravens began to shuffle and complain. Kid covered his ears. Even Tyrod pulled his old hat further down his head. Jude, hunching his shoulders, would have liked to stop Fareed and move out of earshot, but he dare not.

Odd shapes were closing in on the wagon, brushing past him, over him, round him, through him: *things* that were little more than shadows, or shadows within shadows, those creatures usually fleetingly glimpsed only from the very corner of the eye; beings spun from river mist or cloud; creatures whose presence could only be detected by the air shimmering and dancing as they moved. After them trailed familiar smells: the sharp green scent of spring sap rising; the heady perfume of a blow-bell wood; the rich warm odours of sun-baked clay, and that of rain-soaked summer dust; the smoky odour of an autumn hedge bottom; the dank reek of a wet cave; the stench of the pinewoods where small beasts crept to die. On and on they came, until the moment Ersay stopped singing.

Jude glanced back. "What were they?"

"They were …" Ersay hesitated. "They were those beings that unfailingly worked with me rather than against me."

"Oh," said Jude. "Are they real?"

"As real as you may be, Jude." She laughed and Tyrod joined in. Jude glanced at Kid, wondering if he'd got the joke; apparently not, judging by the small shrug. So that was all right then. Jude trudged on, none the wiser. Everything had been so much easier in the old days. Things were, or they were not. Things were solid and had form, or existed only within some fireside story. No point in worrying about any of it, he supposed; just keep walking, and walking, and then walk some more.

When the land finally levelled out, he halted. "We must stop for a while."

"There will be no stopping," declared Tyrod. "Didn't I make myself clear last night, boy? Events are moving too fast."

"Fareed must rest. *I must rest.*"

"Water him. Let him roll. And eat too, if he must. Then we move on."

"Bluddy no!" shouted Jude. He watched as Tyrod fiddled meaningfully with the lapels of his stained blue coat, jumping back horrified as the threat sank in. "All right. *All right*. Don't blame me if the poor bluddy creature drops dead. Or me, for that matter."

"Pfff!" jeered Tyrod. "Good riddance to bad rubbish, I say."

"You ride for a bit," offered Kid, suddenly materialising out of the gloom. "I can look out for holes as well as you."

"It'll be dark soon," Jude muttered, sullenly. "There won't be any moon tonight. You'll have to get *him* to light the way."

"Go on, bluddy rest," insisted Kid. "We can do it by turns. I can soon kick your fat carcass awake if it's needed."

But it was Tyrod who woke him, shaking his shoulder so hard Jude feared he might yank it from the socket.

"On your feet, idler. She has a task for you."

"Uh?" Jude roused himself unwillingly, certain he'd only just dropped to sleep. His feet were sore. His whole body ached. The air was damp and cold. He'd dreamed of falling forever into a bottomless abyss. Sitting up he found himself regarded by a multitude of glowing eyes, with Ersay's face a pale oval against the roof support. Jude yawned again, and replayed Tyrod's words. A task. *The* task. At last! He could do this. Wasn't this what he'd come for? "Yes. Yes. What do you want done?"

"Go deep into the wood. Show yourself to the ancient creatures there. Tell them it is time." Her sweet voice galvanised him into action. And yet, even as Jude leapt to the ground, he frowned. There'd been a quaver beneath Ersay's words that hadn't been there before; a new huskiness. An unnamed fear gathered like a knot in the pit of his stomach.

"How will I find the way?"

"The way will find you."

Jude waited for more, but Ersay said nothing else.

The trees beside the track, softly illuminated by Tyrod, stood as tall and straight as the bars of a cage. With Kid close behind, Jude stumbled deep into the woodland until the light was little more than a dim memory. He stopped.

"What's this about, Kid?

"Don't you know?" He sounded astonished.

Jude scowled. "Would I bluddy ask if did?"

"She is collecting the creatures of the earth to her."

Jude thought about it for a minute. "Why?"

"Don't know." He sensed the usual quick shrug of Kid's bony shoulders.

"It's them holes, isn't it?" A new fear gripped Jude. "They're everywhere. The land has turned sick. Some of it is rotting away. It's dying! Everything's dying. What's going to happen if –"

"Shhh!" hissed Kid. "Shut your face. There's something there."

Holding his breath, Jude became keenly aware of furtive movements and quiet snuffling nearby. They were being circled. Whatever it was could see them perfectly clearly. He grabbed hold of Kid's arm. "What is it?"

"How should I know? Stop that." Kid irritably knocked away his clutching hand. "You know what she said. Get on with it."

"Come with us," Jude gabbled to the empty air. "Come with us now. It's time." His words were greeted with a sound remarkably like a snarl. "*She* says it's time," he amended. The snarls were repeated. Enough was enough. Without waiting to see if the creatures were following, he blundered back towards Tyrod's distant glow. "Brocks!" he said, when they reached the light. "We ain't carrying them. They're bluddy dangerous." Tattow had warned of the damage cornered brocks could inflict. Worse than a stoat, he'd said, bad as the nastiest of dogs. Two winters back, Tattow and Osker had slaughtered an injured one. Even then, its bites had left scars. Ma smoked the hams over an oak fire and – Jude watched uneasily as the brocks sniffed at the hubs – rendered the carcass for wheel grease.

"They need help to enter," said Ersay. "Lift them, Jude."

Jude hung back. Tyrod cuffed him.

"If she says lift them, you lift them. You are her servant, nothing more."

"Why not him?" Jude demanded, indicating Kid.

Tyrod scowled. "She asked *you*. Now, LIFT THEM."

"I don't mind helping," said Kid. Between them they heaved the brocks' stout backsides into the body of the wagon. A soft whirring and chattering followed, and as swiftly died away. A pale night howl drifted down; its plaintive call vibrated on the still air and presently its mate responded. Ersay laughed aloud and mimicked the sound. Small shapes repeatedly skimmed their heads as they set off again. Jude ducked and repeated the charms for dispersing leather-birds.

"Your turn to rest," he told Kid, unwilling to put himself within reach of the brocks' formidable jaws.

Things grew worse as the night progressed. Tyrod's light became steadily dimmer and, as the darkness closed round them, Jude was forced to put his trust in Fareed, knowing that the horse was exhausted, knowing that the smallest lapse of concentration, the tiniest misjudgement, might spell oblivion. Jude's eyes burned from staring so intently at the track. Each step of the journey became a gamble and dawn seemed late in coming. The pale light suddenly died leaving them stranded in the blackest night imaginable but Fareed automatically plodded on, ignoring the staying hand on his throat strap. Perhaps he was sleep-walking. At any rate, the horse mistook the message and put on speed. Terrified, Jude ran after him, hauling so hard on the reins that his heels skidded along the track's surface.

When Fareed finally stopped, Jude's forward momentum made him stumble and fall. And immediately the world skewed and flipped. A dull roar made the air quiver. "No!" Jude rolled into a ball, covering his head with his arms, waiting to be stampeded by the crowds, but this was a different place, one with soft earth that shifted uneasily and was scalding hot beneath his elbows. He slowly raised himself onto his knees. The air tasted thick and vile, each in-breath scorched his lungs. He scrubbed at his eyes, which were so dry and gritty that it was painful to keep them open. Squinting through swollen lids Jude could make no sense of what lay before him: unless he was looking at a sheet of stained canvas, the world appeared matt and flat, monochrome and totally void of movement.

Another bout of intense rubbing brought tears, his eyes adjusted and vision returned. He caught his breath. In every direction the ground seemed to have been baked hard in a pit-kiln with Bett's clay thumb-pots and then pounded into pale dust that constantly moved like solid water into swirls and eddies and ripples. This land was dead. There wasn't a plant or tree in sight, but here and there fountains of thick black goo erupted in a terrible parody of the crystal clear springs that acted like markers along the way to Jude's group in the old days.

In spite of himself, the sight of the black stuff momentarily pleased him and a host of strange images flitted somewhere behind his eyes that made no sense until they somehow meshed with Osker's tales of splendour and riches. And in the far distance, the wasteland was broken up by strange tall structures resembling the tepees sometimes built in the dead of winter when there wasn't enough room for all to sleep in the wagon. As Jude continued to stare, something as soft and wispy as grey thistle-down drifted by and he turned to find its source. It was smoke. Jude jumped to his feet. The horizon was on fire, a vast inferno belching huge scarlet and yellow flames that leaped to burn the clouds, the whole surrounded by billowing black masses that were gradually obliterating the sky, the land, everything.

"What you bluddy doing?" demanded a familiar voice.

"I'm not doing anything," protested Jude, coughing and choking as the smoke swallowed all the air. "None of it's anything to do with me." He raised his head and saw the first grey light of dawn softening the matt black darkness. Kid was standing over him.

"Been having another bluddy loony turn, I suppose. Want me to take over?"

"No."

"Please yourself."

"I'm too tired to rest."

"You're not making sense."

"No." Jude couldn't admit that he feared what dreams might come. "No, maybe not, but I'll keep going for a while longer."

"Are you hungry?" called Ersay. "Would you like breakfast?"

"Yes," said Jude, without looking round. Tyrod reached forward and cuffed him. "Yes, *please*."

They'd reached a place where a stream burst from a bank and fell into a natural pool. Being well-watered, the grass round about was thick and lush. It was a perfect place for Fareed to take rest and refreshment and this time Jude was determined that he should have a proper break. No way was he asking permission. If Tyrod didn't like it, he could do the other thing.

When he'd finished turning the horse loose, Kid touched his shoulder and gave him a look that was all warning. Jude frowned, not understanding. He sank down, glad to take the weight off his feet. And straightaway the stink told him what the other boy had been trying to convey: this morning the heaped fruit was rotten, putrid, both flyblown and maggot ridden. Thankfully, there was also far less than on previous days. Without a word, Kid scooped it up and disappeared into the bushes. Returning, he scrubbed his hands under the running water.

"Wheat, I guess?" he murmured. "Though there's not much left."

Jude nodded, and for a long moment closed his eyes against the world. Finally he forced himself to look at Ersay. She seemed smaller, frailer, and vulnerable where she had once exuded such power. Her hands were speckled with the unmistakeable blotches of old age. The beautiful hair was threaded through with grey. Deep furrows cross-hatched her brow and a web of lines radiated from cheekbone to jaw. And yet she smiled. Jude returned the smile. His body still reacted, even while his heart ached with sorrow. He saw that her dress was now soft grey with a pattern of wind-blown skeleton leaves.

"Are you hungry?" called Ersay, her voice thin and cracked, her head nodding as if from the palsy Ma's Ma had suffered before her passing. "Would you like breakfast?"

"No," said Kid, taking a tiny handful of wheat and passing the sack to Jude, who emptied the few remaining grains onto his palm, then pocketed them. "Thank you. We've had enough."

"What's happening to her?" Jude demanded of Tyrod. And realised he was staring him straight in the eye. He looked down at himself in astonishment. His trousers were halfway up his calves. When he flexed his shoulders, his jacket was tight across the back. And rubbing one hand across his chin, he discovered, of all things, the fuzz of new beard. He'd already realised Kid had grown, but he saw today that those clothes that started comically over-large for the other boy, were now simply a little big. Turning back to Tyrod, Jude saw that he too had grown old. The majestic frame was stooped, causing the great stave to become more prop than weapon. Tyrod's beard had turned white and straggly. So too had his fearsome eyebrows. Even the good eye was a little milky.

"All is as it has to be," croaked Tyrone. He plucked at Jude's sleeve. "A warning. Listen well. When her dress turns black, do not look back. Do not look back. You hear me, boy?"

"I hear you." But what would happen, he wondered, if at that point they were forced to *turn* back.

# 5

The welcome respite from noticeable holes in the earth continued until well on into the morning and, tired though they were, Jude thought that good progress had been made. Then it began again. There were more of them now, and of all sizes, to the right and the left, sometimes forming beaded chains that made tracks impassable, sometimes wiping them out altogether. The dark holes punctuated almost every valley they passed, and pitted many of the hillsides, both near and far. The journey became a succession of stops and starts; Jude was constantly turning Fareed and backtracking to find a new way forward. And to make matters worse, at one place a rough barricade of stone blocks and boulders had been constructed, blocking the way entirely. It was a well chosen spot, a wooded pass between the peaks of particularly steep hills. To go back from here and find an alternative route would take time and energy they longer had. Jude and Kid clambered to the top of the structure and saw the track was a good one in that it continued without any apparent break for as far as the eye could see.

"Suppose we'll have to bluddy move it," Kid said, glumly. "And Tyrod ain't up to helping."

"By *we* I suppose you mean me," Jude retorted nastily. "While you go and hide behind Ersay as usual."

"Bluddy shut yer whingeing, fat arse, and get started."

Jude scowled and began kicking off the topmost blocks. "Mind out the way, Bug-head-skiver."

"Oh, that's bluddy clever, making a new pile right in the middle of the road."

"Shift them then."

"Ain't you got no brains at all underneath that queer hair? It'd take forever. Why not make a space at the side? Ain't so high there and we can push the stones into the wood – out of our way, see?"

There was sense in this but Jude didn't reply. Grumbling and cursing, he began shoving off the outermost stones while Kid rolled them further in amongst the trees. He'd been working for quite a time before it occurred to him that this barrier must have been erected for a purpose. Did it still? Jude stopped and listened, peering into the woodland for ambushers. He stared down the track, looking for any sign of movement. No one appeared, but he was suddenly uncomfortably aware of being observed. Perched up here, not only was he vulnerable, but the wagon was unprotected, too, because Tyrod couldn't be relied on and as for Ersay … well, who knew? Jude eyed Kid, wondering what fighting skills he might possess. Probably none: the little runt was all mouth. He began working faster, sweating profusely, and keeping one eye on the dark shadows beneath the trees as the barricade all too slowly diminished while the invisible threat seemed to increase. His jacket, already too tight, split across the shoulders as he wrestled with an enormous boulder making Jude suddenly acutely conscious of his new strength. What would Tattow have made of it? And what about Ma? With a little pang, Jude acknowledged that she'd have probably gone on roaring and bullying if he'd been three times her size.

Finally, they were down to bare earth and Jude ran at the wagon.

"Let's go!" he yelled, pulling at Fareed's head.

Kid lingered. "What's the rush?"

"I think we're being watched."

"Yah, nothing here – always frightened of bluddy something, you."

"That's right, and usually with good reason, Bug-head."

Fareed proved reluctant to pass through the gap. It was hardly wide enough: young branches were ripped off the side of the wagon as it dragged past the remaining stones of the barrier.

The old man erupted from the trees mouthing nonsense just as Jude finally led the horse back onto the track. He was a fearsome sight, with grizzled hair half-obscuring his face and reaching to his knees, and enormously long nails that constantly raked at the air. He was naked apart from a few filthy rags wrapped more or less around his loins and as he bounded closer, half-crouching, his hands almost skimming the earth, Jude saw that his eyes were wide and mad, his mouth stained purple from eating the last of the autumn's berries. He tried hurrying Fareed, but the stranger moved fast, jumping up to catch hold of the collar and dancing alongside. The horse shied, flicking his head.

"Where she? Where she?"

Jude raised his fist. "Let go!"

"Where she? Enkie see? Enkie see?"

"Bluddy smack him one," yelled Kid.

But Jude couldn't bring himself to land a punch. Instead he pushed hard at the old man's bony shoulder. And again. Nothing would move him. Enkie continued to cling to Fareed's collar, his voice turning ever shriller as he endlessly repeated the question. Suddenly he transferred his grip to Jude's sleeve. "Enkie see?"

The jacket ripped again as Jude yanked himself free. "Get off me. If you mean Ersay, she wouldn't want to see an old loony like you. Touch me again and I'll smash your face."

Enkie continued to run alongside, hopping and skipping as he matched his pace to the slow plod forward of the horse. Jude aimed a kick. He elbowed Enkie as he twirled and jumped. Enkie began to wail, a terrible sound compounded of grief and loss and despair. Jude couldn't stand it: all the feelings he'd suppressed over the loss of his group, his family, were contained in Enkie's long-drawn-out howls of anguish. Again, he raised his fist. This time he would bluddy use it.

"Shut your mouth!" he yelled. "You hear me? Stop your noise right now – or I'll do it for you."

"No more threats are necessary," said Ersay, supporting herself on the frame of the wagon. "I am here." Frail and bent, she smiled down at the wild stranger.

"Ah." Enkie's eyes cleared. He stopped prancing and clapped his hands. "Enkie see."

"Go now, Enkeedu."

"Enkeedu. Yes." Enkie nodded vigorously and patted his breastbone. "Enkeedu."

"Go now. Return to your quiet place with the small creatures among the trees. It will not be for long." Ersay slowly turned and tottered back inside the wagon.

"Enkie see. Enkie see." Enkie laughed and thrust both hands into his mouth. He continued to run alongside until the trees began to thin, then capered away into the wood, his cry of triumph trailing after him.

Jude proceeded with caution. He doubted such a loony could have erected the barricade and if its builders were anywhere nearby they must have been alerted by the commotion. A short distance later they passed the remains of a small settlement tucked into a hollow, pitted with dark holes. It seemed deserted; at least they saw no sign of life as they carefully skirted the outlying buildings. At some time another barricade had blocked the way south, but this had fallen and it was a simple matter to move the few rocks littering the track. Jude breathed a sigh of relief. But then the number of holes suddenly increased dramatically.

Something equally unnerving happened at mid-day, though it took a while for Kid and Jude to notice.

"It's been a fair time since we started going downhill," whispered Kid, coming unusually close.

"Forever," groaned Jude. "How they expect us to …"

"Never mind bluddy whining. Look up."

"What? No. How can I? Take my eyes off the highway for a moment and we could end up falling into nowhere."

"You must," insisted Kid. "It's important. Stop the bluddy wagon, will you? It don't have to be for long."

"All right. What then? Where?"

Kid pointed directly overhead. "See?"

Jude shrugged. "Yeh, it's called the sun. And?"

"And where was it when we started going downhill?"

"You're mistaken," said Jude and started walking again. It was not possible. Therefore he would not think about it. Instead he let his mind roam over old memories and smiled in spite of his misery at the thought of Ma forever insisting he ride whilst the others walked. Well, he'd more than made up for those years of coddling now. She'd thought him precious, believing him the only child in the entire countryside. It was a glorious thing, she'd said, and also a terrible one. Jude imagined her expression on learning that there was another boy, and birthed after him as well. And many more childs too, if Kid was to be believed, imprisoned inside a black city no less.

The thought of Ma and her endless cosseting made him realise that his back was cold. A sharp little wind had risen and was fingering through the tattered jacket. After double-checking their surroundings, Jude stopped Fareed and climbed into the wagon, edging past the sleeping old ones to fumble among the spilled clothes for a jacket that felt big enough. His hands closed on a rough textured one and, even before he drew it into the light, he recognised it as his father's from the carved horn buttons. Ma must have kept it for him. A lump rose in his throat. Something else occurred to him and he looked round, puzzled. There were no creatures in the wagon, nothing at all, only Ersay and Tyrod sunk deep in the slumbers of old age. He emerged frowning, wanting to ask Kid about it, but forgot in the face of the Bug-head's malicious grin.

"Still getting fatter?" enquired Kid.

Jude aimed a blow at the scrawny boy's head, but missed as Kid ducked. He thumped his chest in a gesture that was purely Tattow's. "This is all muscle," he said. "Get off your skinny little arse for once in a while and you might get some."

"Fat," insisted Kid, watching as Jude transferred the contents of his pockets – the perfect apple, mistletoe sprig, toadstool, and winkled the few tiny grains of wheat from a fold in the fabric. "No wonder. Look at all that food."

Jude ignored him. He glanced up at the unmoving sun, and then resolutely faced forward again.

On and on they laboured, down, down, and almost immediately uphill again. There was no avoiding looking skywards as they painfully ascended. Behind the white haze in the west loomed the darkness of the unnatural cloud and when Jude risked a quick peep over his left shoulder, he saw that darkness mirrored in the east, semicircles both, and spreading sideways, like great eyelids, slowly closing. He wondered if the sky was being eaten alive like the earth, and remembered his dream of falling, falling, falling, into a great abyss.

"Fook!" he muttered, his eyes desperately searching the landscape for some safe place to run to.

Kid edged closer. "What's up now?"

"Where shall I start? This feels like the bluddy end of everything."

"Maybe, but Ersay says it is also heralds a new beginning."

"Yeh. Right." Jude ground his teeth. "The bluddy earth beneath our feet is disappearing. Something is swallowing the sky. Sounds like a good place for so-say new beginnings. I wish I'd never started this bluddy journey. What's it all for? If we're finished, why bother?"

"Ersay says," Kid hesitated, "that we two have a part to play in putting everything right."

"Oh, yeh, two fine bluddy heroes us!" It suddenly occurred to Jude that the other boy might know more about the task than he did. He altered his tone. "So what exactly are we supposed to do to save the day?"

"I don't know. Ersay says she will tell me everything I need to know when the time is right."

"Is that so?" Jude said, nastily. Here they went again. Ersay would bluddy tell *Kid,* would she? Bluddy favouritism. Who was it that plodded the bluddy endless miles, always watching the bluddy land for bluddy holes? Who did the bluddy bulk of the bluddy hauling? Who dragged on through the bluddy night while certain bluddy others lay snoring? He did. And was anybody bluddy grateful? Bluddy no. Bluddy Kid got told everything. Not a word to him.

"Ersay says …" began Kid.

"*Ersay says,*" mimicked Jude. "Push off, why don't you." He took a deep breath and launched himself at the hill.

And then came a welcome stretch of flat highway. The few holes were of moderate size with enough level land on either side to negotiate a way round them. By the time the way dipped, it became obvious that Tyrod was well aware that the sun didn't appear to have moved. Rousing himself from apathy he rapped on the wagon with his staff and then used it as a goad for Jude, repeatedly pushing it into his back.

"Lay off," grumbled Jude, moving out of range.

"We should be there by now," Tyrod rasped, his voice cracking with anger, his face reddening. "Faster! Faster!"

"All right. All right," said Jude, forbearing to ask where *there* was. But he made no effort to hurry Fareed who plodded on at the same steady pace until they came to another vast absence in the earth, its dark maw swelling as they watched.

There were more people here, knots of tiny black dots fleeing from the central space, mostly too late and in vain. Jude caught Kid's eye but turned away without comment and began the tedious process of circumventing this lack of place, repeatedly scanning the surroundings for signs that they were being followed.

During that process a pair of cats the colour of twilight shadow sprang at the wagon and clung to the swaying greenery. Ersay cried out in delight, fussing over them like long lost friends. Jude was glad to see them, too: cats were privileged creatures, being bird killers. Not for them, the dark recesses, though: after hissing warnings at the ravens, they made for the box, sitting bolt upright and surveying the countryside with aloof expressions. A couple of dogs arrived too, lean dark creatures with mournful eyes, but Jude hadn't forgotten the earlier attack – besides, he needed to unleash his pent-up rage – and frightened by his hostility, they contented themselves with trotting several paces behind the wagon.

The accident was not so very serious, or wouldn't have been in the days when Jude's group trekked up and down the western boundaries. He half heard Ersay call out, inclined his head to check whether it was him that had been addressed and almost immediately heard a terrible squealing from beneath the nearside back wheel.

"Stop when she tells you to stop!" roared Tyrod.

Rushing to investigate, Jude discovered a small furry creature lying crushed and flailing on the patchy black crust. The dogs sniffed and sprang back, ears down, eyes wary; the ravens clumsily flew down to investigate, shedding a few more feathers.

"It's hurt," said Jude, feeling helpless. "I think its back is broken."

Ersay cried out, and Tyrod's mouth tightened. "Finish it off then."

"I … I can't." Jude stared from the screaming creature to the frantic running backwards and forwards of its mate. He froze. Kid shoved him aside and seized a large stone. The screaming ceased.

"She's more of a man than you are," scoffed Tyrod as the ravens sidled closer.

Jude's jaw dropped.

Kid said nothing.

At the top of another long hill Jude stopped to let Fareed rest, anxious about his laboured breathing. The horse was exhausted; he wasn't taking in enough food and water, but then, none of them were. To his relief the land swept downwards from here, onto a great plain that continued, almost uninterrupted, as far as the eye could see. There would be no more climbing for a while. Immediately below, the track wound through a great forest of autumn gold trees and beyond that loomed the remains of ancient towers.

Ersay was suddenly beside him, groaning with exertion from those few short steps, catching hold of Fareed's harness to steady herself. Jude looked down at her, alarmed, and saw that what Tyrod had warned him of was rapidly coming to pass. Ersay's dress had become a long flutter of tatters, almost completely black, save for a rusty tinge here and there and a scattering of mid-winter berries across her bosom. Round her bony shoulders was draped a shawl, November grey, dappled with shadow, sprinkled with hoar frost. When she turned her face to him Jude stifled his cry of disgust, he forced himself to stand his ground, for all that had been beautiful in Ersay had fled and what remained was truly repellent. Her once lustrous eyes had become dry wells, sunk deep into dark-smudged sockets. The lovely skin was blotched, scored and cracked as parched river bed, dotted with wens, livid with open sores. Pale scalp shone through the scant white hair. The smell of death hung over her.

"I remember this place." There was pleasure in Ersay's thin voice as she regarded the landscape. "In my heart lies the memory of this valley, but the whole of all that was and is and shall be lies lost there within."

She lifted her cramped claw and pointed, directing Jude's gaze to a bright green hill, far away, rising from a boiling sea of mist. On its summit stood a slender tower, exactly as in Jude's dream, except for the absence of a rainbow. Neither was there any cave visible. But the pounding had already begun deep in the ground beneath his feet. Ersay's hand flew to her heart.

"Go," she gasped. "Time is very short now. Go with all speed. And when you get to the hill, follow the seven-fold silver trail right to the top. No shortcuts. Whatever befalls, Jude, whatever goes amiss, you must be sure to follow the trail exactly and take us *all*, every last one of us, to the very top."

"Is that my task?" asked Jude. "Was this journey my task?"

Ersay's smile was a faint echo of what it once had been. "In part. But also, what has been lost urgently needs to be rediscovered."

"What was lost?" asked Jude, baffled. "And when?"

"Answering your own question is part of the task." Ersay patted his arm. "And you, my brave one," she put her face next to Fareed's velvet nostrils and they shared each other's breath, "I give you a little of my remaining strength. Soon it will be your turn to rest."

"But ... but ... what else do I have to do?" demanded Jude.

"I know how much you have yearned to be held, Jude. Do you still want to be held now? Are you man enough yet to kiss this loathly lady?"

Was that also part of the task? Jude took an almost imperceptible step backwards, but Ersay saw, and laughed.

"Not yet, it seems." She held out her hand. "Help me to my seat."

Ashamed, Jude complied, then sank his hands deep into his pockets, feeling like a youngster newly chastised. His fingers closed on something cool and round. It was the perfect apple from the ancient tree by the river, a tree that by now must surely have been erased by the creeping land pox. He wordlessly offered it to Ersay.

"You give me what is already mine, Jude, but I thank you."

Seeing Tyrod watching silently, Jude cast around for a gift for the irascible old man. He had nothing. Then he remembered what had been stowed high in the wall of the wagon and climbed up to retrieve Bett's bag of runes, braving the ravens perched on the greenery above as they lunged forward, beaks stretched wide. Tyrod emptied the rune stones into his shaking hand. He laughed mightily. The slap on the shoulders was a shadow of former blows but it was enough to knock Jude off balance and cause him to fall from the wagon.

"You also have given me what is already mine, boy. The intention was kind though and I thank you. They will be yours again, by-and-by."

And then there was Kid. Jude had nothing at all for him ... *her*. He looked sidelong at her, noticing now what must have been apparent all along, and felt his face flame. The ravens produced loud kronks of derision. Tyrod clapped his hands.

"Come now, save such thoughts for later. Make all speed. The journey is almost over. Then we can begin."

Looked at from above, it had seemed that the worst must surely be over, the rest straightforward. It was not.

Fareed seemed invigorated by Ersay's touch and sprang forward so eagerly that at first Jude struggled to keep up, though Kid, loping along on the horse's other side, managed it easily enough. Down through the soughing trees they ran, and as they passed every tree shuddered and shed its leaves, past the ancient towers, their deep wells of solitude and their many pools of tears, out onto the flat where the land itself seemed to throb and tremble with the quickening beat deep in its core.

"Not much longer!" called Jude, as if to Fareed but with his eyes on the girl. She didn't answer, but tipped her head back, staring straight up to where the sun hung motionless. The black hair gleamed and danced. Even Tattow's bulky old clothes couldn't hide the grace and beauty of her slender limbs. And now Jude knew why Kid had been fought over and a terrible rage grew in him at the remembrance of those glimpses of her bruised and battered body – and admiration, too, for her courage. Kid had survived.

"Whoa!" yelled Kid, and Jude was dragged along the ground as Fareed slowed down. He looked ruefully at his rope-burned hands before glancing around. The gently undulating track had lost its crust and all but disappeared here, shrunk through long disuse until only a faint indentation in the grass remained. It seemed sound enough, though, and the ground was firm. "What's wrong?"

"There," Kid said shortly, and nodded to a line of bare poplars ranged across the near horizon like so many fly whisks.

Once, long ago, Da came by, or perhaps made, a set of nine pins and Jude had spent every stationary hour playing with it until lack of firewood had claimed the pieces in the dead of a bitter winter. These trees went down exactly like the pins, but silently, without the satisfactory series of clicks that came before the tumble. They'd come to another hole in the land.

"We'll have to work round it," decided Jude. "It's all grass here so let's go across at an angle and try again."

And that was easier said than done. As they soon discovered, rather than a hole or hollow, this was a great rift stretching in both directions as far as the eye could see, separating them from their goal. Jude stopped after tramping alongside for a weary distance and still seeing no end to it.

"No point in this."

"It's getting wider all the time," said Kid. "Where now?"

"I'll ask *him*. Perhaps he'll know what to do."

Tyrod was dozing and unwilling to wake. "What? What?"

At some point the dogs had leaped inside to sit with their muzzles on the old man's knee, but they slunk back into the shadowy interior as Jude approached. He hesitated, noticing that Ersay's clothes were now dark as winter midnight, threadbare as cobwebs, only saved from complete blackness by virtue of the uncountable number of dancing, drifting snowflakes, no two the same, decorating the skirt. He also saw that Tyrod's coat hung open, and bent closer only to find that there was nothing within, simply a dark void with here and there the faintest muffled twinkle of …

"WHAT?" roared Tyrod, hastily wrapping his coat around him as the half-feathered ravens stretched out their bare necks and mimicked the sound. "Are we there, huh?"

Jude took a step backwards. "Not yet. A great crack in the earth – there's no way through."

"Find a way," snapped Tyrod. "Of course there's a way. There can't *not* be a way. A way will be left open until she arrives at the place. How could it be otherwise?"

Jude sighed. "Right."

Kid did her usual shrug. "Which way then?"

"I don't know."

"The way we've been going takes us further away from that hill," Kid pointed out, "so we might as well try the other direction."

This was a choice they soon regretted. Where tracks had become strangled with undergrowth, it had been Tattow's job to stride ahead, clearing the way with a lethally sharpened billhook. Jude's small knife was useless here and – though the land was still flat – progress was slow as they were forced to weave a careful path between the huge mounds of brambles, fierce thorn bushes and shoulder-high, steel-barbed thistles that barred their way. And now the sky began to darken. A threat hung on the air. A few spots of rain fell.

Finally they came to a place where a thin bridge of land joined here to there.

Jude took his courage in both hands and walked out a few paces, tentatively testing its strength. "It seems solid, for now, at least."

"Maybe," said Kid, "but it ain't ever bluddy wide enough."

"It's got to be. There's no other way." Jude crouched, carefully measuring in hand widths the space between the outer rims of the wheels. As far as was possible, he did the same with the strip of land, avoiding the extreme edges which wavered and shifted. He tried to avoid looking into the chasm itself, but failed miserably. His eyes were drawn to the profound darkness on either side; it seemed to reach out for him, sweet arms opening promising rest, gentle oblivion, an end to the ache of loss, striving and difficulty. And it was close to the source of the deep pounding beat, he realised, leaning over the edge …

"Well?" demanded Kid, yanking him backwards. "Is it, or ain't it?"

Jude looked at her, momentarily bemused. "Is it what? Oh, yeh. Only just wide enough, though. If we should slip …"

"We won't."

"Let's hope not. All right, here's what we'll do. You guide Fareed. Walk him forward very slowly. Slowly as you can. I'll do my best to keep the wheels on the land. If I shout stop, you stop dead. Understand?"

"I ain't bluddy stupid," snapped Kid.

"No, I didn't mean … Can we just get it over with?" Straightening his back, Jude took one long look ahead. Beyond the other end of the bridge he could see sweet green grass. It was only a few short paces, forty maybe, but it seemed a bluddy long way. "Go!"

Falling to his knees, Jude shuffled forward, matching Fareed's steps and holding the wheels on course by sheer brute force. Cold sweat ran down his forehead and misted his eyes; it trickled vertebra to vertebra, spilling over to finger his ribs. His nose ran, but he dared not wipe it. Terror gripped him each time bits of earth crumbled away, narrowing the bridge still more, and when stones tumbled silently into the abyss, or a clump of daisy root, or plantain. Once – when it was too late to call *stop* – the strip of land abruptly narrowed by almost a wheel's width leaving the rim to hang over the edge; with every ounce of his strength he heaved it back on to solid earth again. They were nearly over, between the wheels Jude could see Fareed's great feathered front feet were within a pace or two of the opposite side, when a small boulder rolled slowly out of the body of the bridge and hurtled downwards leaving a space that somehow the wheel would have to pass over. A scatter of earth followed, then more. And behind him, under his boots, he could feel the whole thing crumbling out of existence. For one horrible moment his left foot hung in mid air.

"Run!" he screamed. "Run him! Quick as you can! It's going."

With a great creaking, the wagon was over. Jude gathered his strength and flung himself full length at the grass. So intense was his relief, that he kissed the earth. And immediately he heard Ersay laugh, a tiny sound as of the rustling of dry leaves in winter that spread out and out like ripples on a pond. Jude hurriedly got to his feet. Behind him the bridge ceased to be with unnerving silence. The land beyond the chasm began to disappear at an alarming rate. He swallowed hard and resolutely faced forward.

"We made it." Kid gave him a swift hug and just as swiftly jumped away.

"Yeh." Jude suddenly felt more cheerful.

"And it's raining," she announced, holding out her hands.

As if on cue, the sky opened. No sweet shower this, no short-lived welcome downpour. Torrential rain fell in a solid curtain, instantly puddling the ground, swirling instead of draining into the soil, lapping at their boots, rising. But at least the conical green hill was no longer far away and since there was no sign of any track, all they could do was make straight for it. The rain continued to empty down as if from a giant trough. Before long, the water was up to their ankles and still rising, and now they saw that the hill they were heading for was surrounded as if by a lake.

Jude groaned. He'd forgotten about the water.

"Get on the wagon," he shouted, going close to make himself heard above the slosh of the wheels, the battering of rain against the remaining canvas.

Kid shook her head. "I ain't sitting up there with those two."

"Climb up on Fareed's back, then. There's no point in both of us wading through this. And I'm taller than you."

By way of answer, Kid ploughed on through the shallows and into the lake. And looking at Fareed, Jude recognised that she was right not to burden him further for it seemed that the old horse's strength had finally deserted him. Mouth gaping he shambled miserably on, plunging and splashing as he pitted himself against the rising water. Jude let him go where he would and fought for his own survival. Twice he stepped into a dip and found himself up to his chest. Once to his chin. He lost sight of Kid altogether. And under his feet, running through his bones and his marrow, he felt the great vibrating heartbeat becoming faster and weaker. When he finally reached the lower slopes of the hill it was so faint that he stood for a moment, fearing it might stop without knowing why he feared.

Then Jude saw Fareed, down on his knees, and Kid struggling under the water to free him of his worn trappings. Like it or not, every occupant of the wagon would have to walk to the summit. Fareed could take them no further.

# 6

The rain stopped as suddenly as it had begun. Jude squeezed the worst of the water from his hair and clothes and stood ankle deep at the edge of the lake staring up at the hill. From here the climb looked far more daunting than seen from afar and whatever his immediate response had been to Fareed's collapse, in his heart of hearts he knew that neither of the ancient ones were capable of scaling those steep sides. There was no sign of Ersay's silver trail – or of any other, for that matter. All he could make out was a series of faint ridges or indentations more or less circling the slopes. Then he caught sight of a broad track half-hidden by a thicket of Slay-thorn and guessed from the angle of its gentle curve that this probably led around the other side of the hill and on up towards the tower.

Heartened, Jude turned back to Fareed. At least now Kid had freed him of the trappings the poor old horse was attempting to rise, struggling to his feet with all the clumsiness of a newly dropped foal. Jude patted his flanks, wishing he had a wizened apple or chunk of root, something, *anything*, to reward this faithful friend for such a long trek. There was nothing. At the thought of food, Jude's stomach growled a long-drawn-out protest. He fished hopefully in a pocket, found only the pitiful pinch of wheat, just seven grains and those spoiled by the rain, damp and swollen and covered with a purplish bloom that made him hesitate momentarily at some deeply ingrained warning struggling to the surface. Whatever it might have been, his hunger won. Still chewing, he pointed out the track to Kid.

"Reckon he'll manage to get us up that after a bit of a rest?"

Kid shook her head. "Not a chance."

"It's not too steep."

"He still ain't up to it. Fareed's done enough. Look at the way his legs is shaking. Poor old bugger kept going till he dropped. Nobody can't ask no more of him than that." She looked from the wagon to the tower, as if measuring the distance. Her chin came up, but he could see defeat written all over her face. "What do we do now, Jude?"

It was the first time she'd used his name. Jude didn't reply for a long moment, wondering why such a small thing should mean so much. What mattered more was that Kid was looking to him for a solution. And that he didn't have one.

"Could we carry them?"

Again Kid shook her head. "Ersay must arrive in her wagon of flowers with her creatures all round her." And truly it was a beautiful sight, massed with sweet scented blossoms – all the flowers of a perfect summer morning, wild roses, honeysuckle, moon daisies, cowslips, purple orchis, kingcups, yellow flags, scabious and hare-bells, more – the whole lot dripping with raindrops that danced and sparkled in the watery sunlight like piled gems in a fireside story.

Jude was silent. Kid continued to look at him. How could he tell her that, with the exception of the cats and dogs – and those filthy birds of Tyrod's – all the creatures had long gone? And that without Fareed there was no way of getting the wagon up to the tower? It was a bitter thing to have come so far and be confronted by failure.

Then suddenly, like a gift, the obvious answer arrived in the shape of a dim memory. Many years ago, soon after the great sickness that resulted in so many bodies being burned along with every last possession, they'd come across a small group of travellers forced into taking turns at pulling their wagon themselves after their own horse had been stolen. Most of those strangers were old and infirm. Weary and consumed with bitterness too, that for all the watching and waiting and privation their travelling days were drawing to a close without a hint of the long-expected sign. They'd sought a final resting place, a safe haven, and the discussions and advice-giving lasted far into the night. Ma had been appalled by their plight, Jude remembered that very clearly, loudly berating them for not acquiring another horse by fair means or foul and Da had only silenced her with difficulty, but if those with failing health could pull a loaded wagon then with any luck …

Jude squared his shoulders. "We should be able to manage it between us. It's the only way." Kid stared. Defeat melted into disbelief. A moment later, she was back on form.

"Are you bluddy mad, fat boy?"

He was no longer fat, far from it, but Jude decided to let that go. No point in trading insults in such a situation. "No, I've seen it done before, Bug-head. Even for a runt like you it won't be so bad once we get the wagon rolling."

Kid stared some more. "I suppose we can try," she said, doubtfully. She looked from the wagon to the hill. "After all, what else is there?"

Jude nodded towards the broad track. "Come on. There's the start of it, no point in standing here, especially when the sky's collapsing and the ground could disappear from beneath our feet at any time."

"Up there?" Now Kid hung back. "But didn't Ersay tell you about the silver trail?"

"There isn't one."

Kid pointed. "What's that then?"

The sun was growing stronger now, battling its way through the cloud. Its rays picked out the raindrops cupped in every leaf, hanging trembling from each blade of grass and from the countless delicate cobwebs clinging to the ridges coiling around the hill. The drops shone with such intensity that the hill looked as if it were encircled by a vast silver-scaled snake. The ridges stood out perfectly clearly now; Jude counted them. There were seven. He was indeed looking at the seven-fold track, exactly as Ersay had described it. And as the sun grew stronger still and the last of the clouds dispersed, there was the rainbow of his dreams, pale as yet, but curving right over the top of the tower.

"Oh," he said. "Yeh, all right, I see it. But we can't pull a wagon along those. They're really steep – besides, they're far too narrow. *And* doing that would make the haul to the top seven times as long."

"Nevertheless," argued Kid, turning stubborn, "Ersay said we must."

"So what?" Jude shifted uncomfortably. No short-cuts, Ersay had insisted, but perhaps she hadn't allowed for the scale of the changes. Now the whole weight of just about everything had come to rest on his shoulders. And there was an urgency about this last phase of the journey that maybe neither of the old ones had foreseen either – the pulse beneath his feet was no more than a flicker, hardly there. He didn't really understand the purpose of climbing this hill, but if it was to somehow save Ersay then all this talking was wasting precious time. He shrugged. "They're asleep. They'd never know."

"I never sleep!" bawled Tyrod. "Am I not Lord of the Heavens?"

"Yeh, yeh," muttered Jude, thoroughly irritated by this voice standing in for his conscience. "And I suppose that's why you sit day and night on your bony old arse doing nothing to help."

"Shhh," whispered Kid.

"Why? What's he going to do?"

"Silence, insolent boy!" bellowed Tyrod. "Do you know who you're talking to? I am the ruler of the skies. I am the summoner of souls and the bringer of victory. Creatures of the earth die, kinsfolk die, you, yourself, shall likewise die, but I shall never die, for …"

"Not doing a very convincing job, old man," jeered Jude, raising his voice a fraction, hoping to coax a conspiratorial grin from Kid, "because from where I'm standing …"

"What's that?" Tyrod hauled himself to the front of the wagon, his near-bald ravens clinging to his shoulders. Old and feeble he might be, but his face was black as thunder, his fury almost tangible, his power indisputable, and Jude took several steps backwards, all the bravado gone. "Then stand no more!"

Tyrod jabbed at the space between them with a fore-finger that glinted silver and Jude clutched his chest as some invisible projectile slammed square into the middle of his breastbone. He heard Kid cry out as his knees started to buckle and through dimming eyes saw Tyrod's finger thrust forward a second time. Jude staggered, fighting to stay upright, but Tyrod's third thrust forced him to the sodden ground.

And Jude was back in the square, kneeling on cold grey stone, curled tight and trying to protect his skull from the ineluctable stampede of the crowd. He stood in the forest clearing, his teeth chattering, his whole body trembling, his stomach heaving at the sounds and the stench and the misery. He knelt in the place where black springs burst through the baking earth. He was in the square. He stood shaking and trembling in the forest clearing. He was …

"No!" One of the wagon's wheels, up to its hub in water, materialised in front of Jude's nose. He caught hold of it, clinging on as the darkness threatened to claim him once more.

"It wasn't me," he shrieked. "I've done nothing."

"Exactly," boomed Tyrod. "You always did nothing."

The wheel popped like a bubble leaving sunlight so bright it hurt. Jude found himself looking down on breathtakingly beautiful forest, stretching as far as the eye could see. This was better. The air was sweet and clear. For the space of a heartbeat Jude felt at peace, but then the noise arrived – a clacking and whirring so loud that he shrank back, terrified – and with it came realisation that his feet had no contact with the earth, he was trapped inside a metal box and the few clouds dotting the brilliant azure sky were below him rather than above. He began to panic, but found himself restrained, unable to rise, unable to turn; there was no escape.

"Road will go through there," crackled a voice in his ear. "Want a closer look? Down we go."

Jude squealed and closed his eyes as the metal box fell through the air. When he opened them again he was hovering over great trees whose crowns were home to chattering animals swinging among the branches, and whose mossy elbows were full of spectacular flowers and strange insects. A flock of monstrous, brightly-coloured, huge-beaked birds arrived and Jude's stomach lurched violently. He closed his eyes. This time when he looked again, the trees had disappeared. All that remained was a wasteland stretching forever into the distance, one of churned mud punctuated by jagged tree stumps.

Jude moaned. The scene shifted. He was back in the square, choking. He was somewhere new, an evil place: the air was tainted and for as far as he could see the land was broken up by foul pits full of liquid the colour of ripe pus; above them loomed great chimneys pumping sulphurous smoke into a charcoal grey sky. And then, in a place bereft and hopeless where the wind howled and grieved over parched countryside. He watched the light dim in the eyes of a woman who begged in vain for water. All around her, bodies, emaciated as Osker's, lay where they had fallen. And then he fell too, into a place where a furious battle raged around him, where the faces of the participants were contorted with hate, where flies feasted on spilled entrails and the gutters ran with blood.

He was back in the square.

He was somewhere else, watching a huge cloud rise far off, its top spreading until it hung motionless like a great white tree.

He was in the forest clearing ...

And now he was alone, standing on a hilltop surrounded by familiar green countryside with gentle valleys and ancient meadows broken up by the darker hues of woodlands. Before his eyes patches of grey erupted, small at first, rapidly growing and becoming cross-hatched with stripes of black. Jude saw that, as in Bett's stories an enchantment lay on the land for there was no stopping the growth of this hideous greyness. Turn where he would, like the angry red around the swollen core of a boil on a body covered with many boils, the patches of grey spread relentlessly outwards until they met with others, forming a bigger mass that in turn swelled further and joined others until hardly a speck of green countryside remained. Jude shuddered at the ugliness of what remained. He shuddered at the memory of all that he'd seen. He knew these things were wrong but couldn't see how they were connected. Finally it came to him: they were situations created by men that had gone before. And, though he didn't understand, his heart told him that somehow these were sins perpetuated against Ersay.

"What do you say now?" roared Tyrod

"I didn't do any of those things!" protested Jude. "It wasn't me."

Tyrod stood before him, tall, majestic, in his prime. "All this was done to her by mankind. Instead of honouring her, instead of thanking her for their very forms and their sustenance, they've done nothing but rape and pillage."

"But not by me! It had nothing to do with me."

"The child is father to the man," said Tyrod. "Through many lives you had the chance to play your part. Now you are the scapegoat, the holy fool. By taking on the task you take on the crimes of your fellow men. Perhaps in redeeming yourself, you will redeem your race." His mouth twisted into a sneer as he looked Jude up and down. "There again, perhaps you will not."

"What is the task?" asked Jude, his voice hoarse with fear as he swallowed the insult. No answer came.

He blinked, and there was the wagon wheel, his fingers still clinging to the spokes. Kid stood over him, frowning. Tyrod was slumped on the box, his mouth open and his eye vacant. As Jude struggled to his feet, Tyrod also hauled himself upright, grunting and wheezing, holding out his arms for the ravens as they flopped clumsily down from the roof.

"What happened?" whispered Kid. "Who were you talking to?"

"I saw things ..." Jude shook his head, attempting to get his thoughts in order. "Tyrod. He showed me things. Terrible things ..." He shuddered. "I can't explain. You wouldn't understand."

"Why not?" And when he didn't answer, Kid shrugged and picked up one of the shafts. "Fine, keep your little secrets. If we're going to try this, then we'd better get going. I don't know how long Ersay's got."

And Jude realised he could feel no pulse beneath his feet. He steeled himself to look inside the wagon. Ersay's dress had turned completely black, draped across her skeletal form like a gauzy veil. Both cats still sat aloof but the dogs lay with their heads on Ersay's knees, staring with mournful eyes at her blotched and ruined face. Jude thought her dead, there was no perceptible rise and fall to her chest, no movement of any part of that gaunt frame, but she opened her eyes as Tyrod shuffled back inside pushing contemptuously past him.

"It is time." Her whisper sounded like wind through winter-dry grass. "Come to me. Come to me now. It is time."

Tyrod grunted. "Mother of all, we come." He thrust forward his arms forcing the two ravens to spread their sparsely feathered wings and shuffle their feet as they struggled to balance.

"Ah." Ersay eased herself into a sitting position, propped against the side of the wagon among the clusters of apple blossom, wild roses and white thorn that had worked their way through the living wattle walls. The flower-scented air vibrated as she spread her hands and took a long, deep breath. The ravens disappeared. One minute they were there, ugly as sin and twice as nasty, the next they'd gone, simply ceased to be. The cats and dogs too ...

Jude hurriedly backed away without waiting to see whether or not Tyrod himself remained.

"Yeh, you're right, we must go now, straight away. And don't forget that we mustn't look back." He grabbed Kid's shoulder, suddenly afraid. "Whatever happens, do not look back."

Kid irritably shook his hand off. "Yeh, yeh, all right, I know that – no need to keep on."

Together they pulled on the shafts. The wagon was far heavier than Jude had imagined. It barely moved half a pace forward before slipping back again, sinking down into the soft mud.

"Try again," said Kid, bracing herself. "It'll be a lot bluddy easier once we get the bluddy thing on solid ground."

Heaving and grunting with exertion, they got the wagon moving, inching it forward out of the water-logged ruts, straining every muscle to stop it rolling back, and finally, with a supreme effort, hauled it onto the grass at the foot of the hill.

"Rest a minute," said Jude, glancing at Kid's white face. She was too small for such work, too slight. "You push and I'll pull," he suggested. "Go to the back of the wagon. But walk backwards to get there, don't turn round." It was as he'd suspected: the job of getting the wagon up the hill was to be his alone. And he was so hungry, so very hungry, almost faint with hunger. The bit of wheat hadn't made the slightest difference. How could this be done on an empty stomach?

His hand crept into his pocket and his fingers closed on the bug-agaric, the red-and-white spotted toadstool so highly valued by Tattow. Jude recalled his anxious scouring of birch copses in search of them; he remembered him lovingly drying them late at night over the dying embers of autumn fires. He chewed cautiously on one small chunk, then his hunger got the better of him and he crammed the whole thing, stalk and all, into his mouth. Why Tattow had prized the things as a delicacy was beyond him. In times of real hunger, Ma had sometimes given him strips of leather to chew on. This had no taste and much the same texture.

"Remember – don't look back," he called to Kid, realising that now he himself could not turn around to check if she was all right. If anything happened to Kid …

"I heard you the bluddy first time," came back the answer.

Jude grinned and wound the ropes tightly round his waist and shoulders before lifting the shafts. The task before him seemed impossible. To move the wagon on flat roads was one thing, to haul it up a hillside quite another; he doubted whether even Da and Tattow could have managed it between them. But there was no one else to help, no one at all. He chomped savagely on the toadstool, baring his teeth, feeling his mouth fill with saliva, holding it there as though swallowing had ceased to be automatic. When he did, his head swam and Jude tensed, afraid of being plunged back into his nightmare visions, forcing himself to focus on the way ahead. But then new strength flowed through his veins. Even though his reach was only just wide enough to take both shafts, somehow he managed to get the wagon moving and it slid forward relatively easily. Everything suddenly became clear. Fook Tyrod and his sneers! He could do this. He could undertake any task that Tyrod burdened him with. Jude saw that the silver trail wound upwards from a huge boulder at the top of a slope and heaved the wagon towards it with such vigour that he failed to see other stones lying alongside, half hidden in the grass. The undercarriage jammed on the biggest, so that for a moment it lodged there, wheels spinning in mid-air; it came free in a rush with a long shriek of protest.

"What the fook was that?" Kid's voice sounded small and far away.

"Nothing important." Jude had other things on his mind. Never mind not looking back, to look forward was terrifying enough: the hill itself now seemed to be floating in a sea of blackness whose waves might even now be eroding the track behind them. He put his head down and increased his pace.

"Not so bluddy fast!" yelled Kid.

Jude didn't answer. He needed every bit of strength he possessed to create some sort of momentum for this was where the climb proper began.

Close to, the ridges were wider than he'd expected; even so it was necessary to walk almost sideways in places, and pull the wagon at a precarious angle, too. He continued to chew at the toadstool. It brought some comfort. At least he no longer felt hunger pangs. Gradually the leathery mass began to soften and maybe Tattow had been right, maybe there was some magic in the stuff for all his tiredness fell away and, although it still required great effort, the weight of the wagon seemed to diminish and his steps grow longer. Up he went, hot and panting, wanting to glance back, needing to check that Kid was still with him, that she was safe, but afraid of what such an action might cost them all.

"All right, Bug-head?"

"Slow down, fat boy."

The track seemed to go on for ever, rising, sometimes falling a little before gently rising again, always coiling around the sides of the hill. His limbs began to twitch and burn. His shoulders ached and the rough jacket chafed his skin. The visions edged closer and Jude fought to keep his attention fixed on the way ahead – on each blade of grass reflecting light from its knife-sharp edge, on the tiny spiders' web mazes hung with glistening beads, and on the silver on silver leaves of Bett's healing Rock Rose that grew so prolifically here – and toiled on sure that he must almost be at the top. Sure too, that it would be too late, that Ersay had gone, that he had failed. Beyond that ... could there be anything beyond that?

A sudden fear gripped him. "You still there, Kid?"

"There's nowhere else left to go, fat boy."

It was a relief to hear her voice, for all that it sounded faint and distant. "Don't look back," he shouted. "Whatever you do, don't look back. Not long now."

"Don't stop," she replied. "Whatever you do, don't give up."

It was timely advice for in front and to one side of the track lay a large moss-blotched rock that seemed familiar. As he came closer Jude saw other stones, half hidden by the rough grass. To his horror, he realised that in spite of the agonised effort, his screaming muscles and breaking back, all he'd done was drag the wagon full circle to the point at which they'd started, only a few paces higher up. He groaned. In front of him the silver trail led on and disappeared round the side of the hill. Six more circuits must yet be endured. And he was on fire. He couldn't breathe. His head spun. Jude rolled the masticated fungus to the side of his mouth and gulped at the damp air. It wasn't enough. He needed to open his jaws wide, to take in great lungfuls of the stuff, and that couldn't be done round a great wad of food – but once again there was this curious reluctance to swallow which he had to fight to overcome. The minute he did, more strength flowed into him. Again his vision sharpened so that small things sprang into focus: the ponderous negotiation of a root by a black beetle; the slow sway of a snail's horns as it moved through the forest of grass; a tiny seed pod springing open. As Jude strained and heaved, attempting to create a rhythm out of brute force, the sun beat down upon his head and beneath his feet the silver snake began to ripple and writhe, growing so bright that it dazzled his eyes.

And then Jude heard a terrible sound, a sound that he'd learned to dread on the open road – when it meant several days of Tattow cursing and axing and hammering – but which must spell the end of everything here. Only a slight sound at first, then louder, louder again, a scream wrenched from the heart wood as the wagon's axle-tree cracked and split. The timber dragged along the grass for a few paces before digging in and twisting, wrenching off the wheels one by one, until the whole weight of the wagon dropped onto the ground forcing him to a standstill.

"Jude!" wailed Kid.

"It's all right," Jude shouted, gritting his teeth as he hoisted the shafts higher. The wagon would be lighter now, little more than an over-large wicker storage hamper without that solid wood under-carriage. Or a sleigh; in the past he'd seen travellers pulling wheel-less sleighs. If it could be done, he would do it. At the very least, he would do it until he could do it no more. Nothing else remained.

Once again he strained forward, pitting his strength against gravity, his heart a great fist beating its way out of his chest, each in-breath ragged and loud. The sweat poured into his eyes. He could no longer see, but did not seem to need to, for his feet unerringly found the path. In places, what was left of the wagon slewed sideways and yet it did not turn over. It did not fall. The burning sensation returned. His whole body was on fire, making him want to leap and run, to fly, but Jude was constrained by the weight at his back. His shoulders had been rubbed raw by the ropes; he could feel blood soaking into the cloth. Splinters from the shafts had worked deep into his palms. Every muscle and sinew ached.

And now, although he could no longer see the snake, he could hear its sly whispers, its breathless promises. Some of Jude's fantasies returned, of epic battles, heroic deeds, and great rewards, of beautiful women, *a* beautiful woman … but at the back of his mind a question began to form and grow, demanding an answer. He turned from it, emptying himself of all thoughts, fixing his eyes on the steadily rising blur of silver that was Ersay's seven-fold path, dutifully keeping going just as poor old Fareed must have kept going year after year.

Without warning, the ground levelled out. Kid was suddenly beside him, helping to support one of the shafts. "Hey – not far to go now, fat boy. We made it! We're almost there."

Jude merely grunted. He had no energy left for anything else. The wagon suddenly lightened; it seemed to float behind them as if it were built only of its shell of flowers, as if it were empty of nothing but an idea. He plodded grimly along the path as it made its final circuit and stopped abruptly by a large smooth stone some thirty paces away from the tower – which was nothing like the graceful structure glimpsed in his dreams. Little more than a roofless, crumbling ruin remained, a broken jag of hollow tooth sticking up from the hill. His spirits plummeted. He'd achieved it, brought the bluddy thing here against all the odds, and not even a thank you. He was thirsty; his lips were dry and cracked. He craved water but there was no sign of a spring. And the question reasserted itself as Jude stood easing his bruised shoulders, head down, biting back tears of exhaustion. What now?

It wasn't really a question, more a realisation. If Tyrod and Ersay held him responsible for all that he'd been shown then the final part of the task could surely only mean one thing: punishment, his death.

# 7

Jude wasn't left to ruminate for long. After a long hard stare, Kid prodded him in the ribs, unerringly picking a spot rubbed raw by the shaft. "What's the bluddy matter now?" she demanded.

"Nothing."

"Oh," she said. "'Cos for a moment there I thought you was going to start grizzling."

"Lay off," snapped Jude. He blinked as the tower receded and advanced repeatedly and at an alarming rate. When it steadied, he saw that it was no longer possible to see through it. Now its hollow centre had been filled with intense midnight black, not a single ray of the brilliant sunlight seemed able to pierce the dense shadow there. And yet ... yes, he was sure something that should therefore have been invisible was moving inside that darkness. He squinted against the light, turning his head this way and that, as if by doing so he could catch a glimpse of whatever it was at the pinpoint corner of his eye. That, Bett said, was the only way to catch otherworldly things unaware. "Kid, can you see ...?"

"Seen you was about to have a blubbing fit. Never mind looking at me like that – it wouldn't be the first time." There was sly laughter in Kid's voice but not in her eyes. "We're here, Jude. We made it. You should be pleased, not acting like someone's chucked you a bone what's had all the marrow sucked out of it." She touched his arm. "What's up? Tell me."

Jude looked down at her slender brown hand. It was filthy, the nails were bitten down to the quick, the knuckles scraped raw, and yet in this moment it seemed utterly beautiful to him. This close, he noticed for the first time that her eyes were a dark storm grey, almost brown, her lips full and soft. Her skin was the glowing deep gold of moorland honey. And it was too late to tell her these things. It was all too late. He swallowed hard. "I'm going to die now, right?" For the space of a heartbeat her face softened. Jude thought he saw compassion there and was filled with longing – to hold her close, to share the burden of his fears and blot out the loneliness which gnawed away at his soul much as the darkness swallowed up the land. He made a small sound, took one tiny step towards her, but the moment passed. Kid snatched her hand away, jumped back, and raised her eyes to the heavens.

"One way journey, ain't it?" She was making fun of him again. He could hear it in her voice. "We was always going to die, fat boy. You surely ain't as stupid as you look, so you must have known that from the beginning."

"I thought ..." Jude shook his head and put his heroic fantasies from him. Clearly he'd imagined that moment of gentleness. Kid was as she'd always been. No point in giving her additional ammunition even at this late stage. "What's it all bluddy been for then, this endless struggling to get here, on and on and bluddy on, going without food and rest, and ...?"

"Well," Kid's shoulders lifted in that characteristic little shrug that mocked him, herself, and the whole wide world that had fallen out of being, "from what you told me it weren't so very different from what you always done year in, year out with your group. Come to think about it, ain't so very different from what anybody ever done, however you dress their lives up."

Jude shifted uncomfortably, only realising now how well he'd been protected by Ma and the others. And maybe they'd also protected themselves from the futility of it all by believing so strongly that they had a purpose, that of waiting for the sign. "But to go through all that just to die at the end of it?" His legs started to twitch and burn again, even more fiercely than before so that he was briefly forced to hop from one foot to the other. And, even worse, he was almost sure that the ground itself was beginning to move, but it was hard to be sure because his eyes had taken on a life of their own and he couldn't stop them rolling around in their sockets. He waited until the sensations died away then sneaked another look at the sunlit tower. The arch was still choked with dense shadow.

"Yeh," Kid laughed out loud. "Born, grow, shrivel up, die. What else is there?"

"Right," said Jude, sourly. "And now *die* is all that's left. Wonderful."

Kid's eyes flashed. "Look, fat boy, we both chose to come here. It was you what turned the wagon round that day. Nobody made you do it. I could have jumped out then, and all. We both had our reasons. Don't really matter though. Fact is, one way or another we'd have been dead already if we hadn't. So when you're done being sorry for yourself, we'd might as well finish what we started. We still got to get Ersay into that there tower."

"Why?"

Kid didn't meet his eyes. "You had your visions," she muttered, "and I had mine. Just do it."

"Right," Jude hesitated, "so … reckon it's safe to look back now?"

"I did, and I'm all right."

"Matter of opinion, Bug-head," said Jude and turned around very cautiously. To his horror, what was left of the wagon lay tipped to one side, battered and broken on the stony ground. Worse, it was almost flat. The roof had collapsed, the sides caved in, and most of the flowers trailed crushed and bruised along the path behind it.

"Oh, fook!" yelled Kid.

Jude covered the distance in two enormous strides. "Ersay!"

"It wasn't like that when I looked just now," gabbled Kid, as they both frantically tore away the wattle panels and creepers. "Some of the flowers had fallen off, but them walls was up and the bluddy roof was still on."

"It can't have been." And yet she must be right: Jude knew that he couldn't have hauled it up the hillside in this state. The shafts were off, the box in pieces, and the ropes were frayed down their entire lengths and partially untwisted at the ends.

"Bluddy was," insisted Kid.

Jude said nothing. Their eyes met as they lifted the last panel. The wrecked wagon was empty. A few rags remained; some leaves, scatters of fur, a handful of snapped off flower heads; nothing else.

"No." Kid walked the length of the wagon, picking up the rags and shaking each one as if in hope that someone might be concealed beneath them. "No. They can't have gone – not now. Don't make sense."

"She must have fallen out," said Jude, cursing at his own clumsy carelessness. He picked up some of the rags, saw they were all that remained of Ma's precious hand-fasting quilt and smoothed them between his hands. "When the wagon hit those stones, or perhaps when the axles snapped."

"I would have seen," insisted Kid. "Think I'm blind, or what? Don't forget I was walking right behind the bluddy thing pushing it. I'd have noticed a bluddy mouse sneaking out, never mind Ersay. And anyhow, with the gob he's got on him, Tyrod would have soon let us know about it if he'd fallen out."

Jude shook his head. "Tyrod probably wasn't there. I think he'd already ..." He thought back to that moment when Ersay had breathed in and the ravens, cats and dogs had disappeared. "I think he'd ... well, *gone* before we started the climb. Most of the other creatures went earlier."

"I could have told you that – too bloody quiet in there for a start. They never stayed long: wasn't room. I asked Ersay about it and she said ..."

"Never mind starting all that *Ersay said* business again," Jude interrupted, wearily. "The point is there was nothing else left in the wagon. Even if there was, seems to me that it's only Ersay we've got to worry about. I'll have to go back and find her."

"Go back where?" Kid whispered. "There's nowhere left."

And now Jude forced himself to look at what he'd been carefully avoiding. He saw that the lower slopes of the hill were no more. Most of the silver trail had disappeared. All that remained was the flattened top of the hill, a perfect circle of wiry grass with outcrops of stone here and there, and the ruined tower at its centre. Beyond stretched a great void, an abyss. Above, the sun turned incandescent, so bright that it was impossible to see what had happened to the sky. Jude ground his teeth. Their whole world had gone into the darkness and it had taken Ersay.

"This happened because you looked back too soon," he snapped. "I bluddy told you not to, again and again."

"Fook you," said Kid and stalked off to the other side of the tower.

Jude sank onto the ground next to the remains of the wagon, wishing the words unsaid. That had been stupid. No good blaming Kid. This was his fault. He'd taken too long over pulling it up the hill. It was his fault that it was smashed up, too. Tattow had drummed into him often enough that once any part of a wagon was damaged it needed mending straight away, leave it and the whole thing would fall to pieces, sooner rather than later. He should have tried to fix the axle-tree – no, stopping for repairs was impossible in those circumstances – but at least he should have noticed those boulders in the grass.

Reaching out, Jude gathered a handful of crushed flowers, the last the earth had to offer, and breathed in their sweetness, remembering Ersay at her most beautiful. What did it matter what became of him? He would have given his life without question for her and yet, not only had he failed in the task, but he'd failed her. Jude wept a little.

Through the mist of tears the tower looked perfect, taller with windows and niches containing statues and, close-by, the fuzzy outline of a larger building. For a moment the carving around the arched entrance itself stood out sharp and clear, three-fold, giving the impression of an arch within an arch within an arch, an entrance leading to infinity. The dense shadows inside had gone. Now, the interior blazed with light and figures passed to and fro. He had an impression of feasting and dancing, as in Osker's stories of courtly love and great adventures. Jude rubbed his eyes and the arch turned grim and dark again. The thick, sooty black shadows of shadows returned but now Jude thought he could make out scarlet and white *somethings* forever coiling and twisting within them.

Kid stood just beyond the tower, head down as if lost in thought; from this distance she looked small and vulnerable and very alone. Jude was tempted to run to her and make things right, but as he knew full well, go closer and she was likely to turn into a wild thing with a tongue as sharp as Ma's.

He stopped watching her when his body began to cry out for water. Jude could never remember being so thirsty. Even on those rare occasions when the water barrels ran dry, there'd always been a stream or spring within easy walking distance. Here there wasn't even a muddy puddle. He parted the long grass searching for a few last raindrops – nothing, the fierce heat of the sun had claimed every last one. Not that it really mattered with the darkness steadily creeping closer since, as far as he knew, the dead had no need for food or drink. He resignedly thrust his hands into his pockets, where his fingers closed on the small spray of mistletoe he'd picked from that apple tree by the great river. The leaves were already crisp and dry, yellowed, crumbling at his touch, but the berries were plump and showed no sign of withering.

Jude tried to remember why this plant had been so important to his group in the old days. Bett sometimes called it All-heal, but she called many wayside herbs by similar names and he'd never seen her use mistletoe to heal anything except nightmares. It must have had other uses too, secret uses that provoked much laughter. Mistletoe treated something of greater importance than cuts and bruises, she'd said, when he asked, something far more essential. And then Bett laughed mightily, refusing to elaborate and leaving him more confused than ever. Even if Jude hadn't understood the cause, he remembered them all searching far and wide for the plant when he was very young and Da and Hew – Bett's man – were still alive. There'd been talk of a playmate in those days, hopes for a new last child, and for a time he'd expected one would be discovered concealed in the largest of the clumps. But Hew had died, and then Da, and with them the urgency of the search. Now he pulled off the pairs of moon-white berries and shovelled them into his mouth, anticipating a few precious drops of juice, but the pulp was viscid and slimy, clinging to his lips and tongue like strings of snot, sliding down his throat. His gorge rose as he tried to scrape the stuff off. A moment later he vomited, bringing up a mass of undigested toadstool.

"Secret eating again?" enquired Kid.

"Fook off," groaned Jude. He sprang up and moved away, still scrubbing at his tongue. "Leave me alone. Why don't you stay that side of the tower and I'll stay this?"

"I would, but not for long. I ain't here for fun. Think I want to be anywhere near a puking, twitching, blubbing loony like you?" And when he didn't respond, Kid continued: "This here last bit of earth – it's being swallowed up extra fast by the dark. Are you listening, fat boy? I said it's all going to disappear bluddy soon."

"I heard." Jude hardly reacted, being preoccupied with something even more immediate. The pieces of that half-understood puzzle suddenly all fell into place. He now knew precisely what had caused Ma and Bett's ribald laughter as they brought home the mistletoe. The effect on his body was all too evident: having four limbs on fire and twitching had been bad enough, but now the fifth was standing rock solid. This was worse, or maybe better, than any secret weaving of hard-breathing fantasies. Face flaming, Jude surreptitiously pulled down his jacket, wishing for a dark corner and hoping Bug-head wouldn't notice. "And? Nothing we can do to stop it."

"*And* I think we should bring what's left of the wagon right up to the tower."

"No," said Jude, still tugging uncomfortably at his jacket. "Have another go at yanking my arms out their sockets? Not bluddy likely."

Kid glared at him, fists akimbo. "You got something else better to do whilst you're waiting to be snuffed out?"

"Why bother?"

Her eyes narrowed. "Because that's what we was supposed to do, fat boy, not dump it all that distance away. State she was in, how could Ersay walk from there? Anyway, they disappeared before and came back again. Remember when that dog-pack attacked us? What if she comes back right when the wagon's falling over the edge of the hole? What then? No, we got to take it up the rest of the way. If you're too fat and lazy to bother, I'll do it myself."

"Like to see you try," sneered Jude. He waited for a moment, getting his body more or less under control by thinking of every sad, bad, and then humiliating thing that had ever happened to him, before following her.

What was left of the wagon looked even worse now that it was covered with dying brown plants. Kid silently wrestled the collapsed wall panels into a single pile on what had once been the floor. She bent over, straining to move it forward, letting fly an unpunctuated stream of what Jude had previously understood to be very bad words indeed as it stuck fast. Her tunic rode up revealing slender back, the sweet curve of her waist and below it the suggestion of swelling hips ... Jude moistened his dry lips.

"What the fook are you looking at?" she snarled.

Jude felt himself flush scarlet. In a feeble attempt to turn his staring into a joke, he muttered: "Dunno, was trying to decide." His sniggers were cut short by a kick that landed square on his knee but which he was sure had been aimed a fair bit higher. "What was that for?"

"You bluddy know," said Kid. "Now help me with this. We ain't got much time."

Between them they cobbled what was left of the ropes into two fairly equal lengths. These they wrapped round the pile of wattle panels, binding them fast to the wagon's floor with creepers. The blazing sun continued to beat down on them, its light a fierce bright white, its heat intense. Once again Jude's limbs felt as though they were on fire; he feared that any moment now, the twitching and jumping and eye-rolling would start again. In an effort to cool down, he threw off his jacket and, after a moment's hesitation, Kid did the same. Her tunic was ripped and sagged forward at the neck. Jude, fighting to keep his eyes on his work, found that by angling himself carefully he was rewarded with brief glimpses of the top of Kid's small breasts. On the pretext of easing his aching back, he stopped and stood transfixed by the beads of sweat rolling down from her neck to disappear into the shadowed hollow between …

"Get on with it," growled Kid, "unless you want another kick."

"Yeh. Right." With a wounded sigh, Jude went back to sorting through the tangled creepers searching out the most supple and using these to whip the holding ends of the ropes. Finally the thing was as secure as they could make it.

"Slowly now," said Jude, taking up one of the ropes. "Don't try and rush. No sudden movements. Not much strength left in the ropes and those creepers could snap at any time." He pushed up his sleeves as he spoke, and saw to his horror that his forearms had turned a sooty purple-black. Jude swallowed hard and tentatively pulled up the hem of his trousers. His legs were the same: black, as though burned, charred.

"What the fook done that?" demanded Kid, wide-eyed. She quickly inspected her own arms. "I ain't got it. That ain't bruises. What is it?"

"Don't know. It's too late to matter. Pull on three. One, two, three …"

Together – shuffling backwards – they dragged the remains of the wagon up the gentle incline to the tower, moving cautiously, edging it on a hand span at a time. It was only thirty paces but seemed to take forever. The creepers snapped. The rope frayed and fell apart. Finally they were on their knees, tugging on clumps of grass to move forward while pulling only on the bare knots attached to what was left of the frame, and then the frame itself.

There was a wide stone step in front of the arch and here they stopped. Without so much as a word, Kid slipped into the shadowed interior. Jude straightened, looking ruefully at his raw palms. He pulled his sleeves down to cover the blackness of his skin and wished that the whole bluddy thing was over. The end was a foregone conclusion. There was no escaping it. Since they were going to die, let it be quick. He took out the fragments of quilt, smoothed them again, bade a last silent farewell to Ma and with a final sigh tucked them inside his tunic.

There was very little land left around the tower now: the darkness was closing in fast. Earlier, Jude had thought that he'd felt the ground moving beneath his feet. Now, he was sure of it. There was no wind; the air was still and heavy, yet all the grass was in motion, swirling into a spiral pattern that looked like the shell of a gigantic snail but which Jude suddenly realised mirrored the seven fold path he'd battled his way around. The hilltop was spinning like a great green wheel with the tower as its hub. They had reached the end.

Jude wondered if Kid would come close for these final moments. He peered into the darkness but could see no sign of her and there was no response when he called her name.

He wondered why they'd bothered to make this final effort and kicked morosely at the heap of broken wattles, noticing as he did that a few wild roses had opened along a length of withered briar, that once again the irrepressible honeysuckle was sending out sappy green tendrils and that wood lilies were pushing between the crumbling staves. Jude's eyes nearly started from his head: Ersay lay amongst them, small and frail, curled in the birth-death position.

"Kid!" he yelled. Still Kid did not emerge. He fell to his knees. "Ersay ..." Wherever she'd been, the old one was still alive: her hands and eye lids fluttered. Jude lifted her very gently and with reverence. She was almost weightless. "Ersay, we are here, at the tower. What must we do now?"

"Ah, there you are, Jude," whispered Ersay, the brightness of her eyes at odds with the papery yellow wrinkles. "Now, are you ready for your task? Are you ready to go in search of what has been lost?"

Jude nodded. "But what ..."

"You'll know it when you see it." Ersay laughed; the sound was wind playing through winter-bleached grass. She laid her withered claw on his hand. "And are you ready to give me that kiss now? In return I will give you the means of answering all your questions and questioning all your answers."

This time Jude didn't hesitate. He didn't want to feel ashamed again and it could be no worse than kissing Ma's Ma on her deathbed. He closed his eyes, and touched his lips to each of her cheeks, her brow, and then, remembering Ersay as she was, he kissed her full on her sunken mouth. He heard her laugh again, louder, more joyfully, and before he knew what was happening she'd slipped from his arms, quick and slippery as a young trow-fish beneath a waterfall.

And when he turned to look for her, Jude caught his breath, staring in disbelief at what confronted him. The outlines of the tower quivered, almost fluid, but the three figures standing in the triple archway were clear enough. Ersay was on the right, an ancient and bony hag, stooped and grizzle-haired, her scanty rags revealing far more of her body than he wanted to see. In the centre stood Ersay, the tall and beautiful woman of his first visions, wearing a dress of green – patterned all over with soft spring flowers – that concealed a great deal more of her lovely form than he would have wished.

The fierce mistletoe-born desire returned as he gazed hard at her. Jude's heart raced, his breathing grew heavier and once again he felt the colour rush to his face. A plaited golden cord lay draped over one of her palms and as Ersay came close she gently placed it around his neck. Jude didn't understand its purpose, but knew that he'd come to the moment he'd longed for, when Ersay would finally hold him in her arms and shower him with kisses and caresses. He reached out, but having fastened the cord, Ersay stepped away from him so that his hands closed on empty air.

And now Jude saw that by her side stood a third Ersay, one that Jude had never seen before, sweet and slender, far younger, a beautiful young woman, a golden-hued girl hardly full grown, and completely naked. He gulped as she stepped forward – leaving an image of herself behind, or perhaps that was someone else, but at any rate holding out her arms to him – for her eyes were not those of a child but held within them knowledge of all the secrets he longed to experience. Scented roses had been woven into her hair. When he touched them the thorns drew blood. All that was left of Ma's quilt fell to the ground between them.

The air thickened. Shadows deepened around them.

Jude forgot the onlookers as the girl-Ersay's long hair enclosed them, becoming a curtain behind which they were hidden; moment by moment its colour changed, sun gold to midnight and back again. They lay together on the sun warmed earth, and by turns her face was Ersay in full bloom, the Ersay freshly budded … and suddenly, when it was too late to matter, it became Kid's. Above them the tower shifted and groaned.

A few lumps of mortar fell. Several hit Jude's back. He hardly noticed as what had always previously been a private golden purr of pleasure built into something wild, frenzied, scarlet-coloured, sucking out his soul, turning him into a being of raw sensation, but one from whom all survival instinct had fled, so that just at the moment when scarlet turned white-hot, gathering in Jude's loins like a mighty unstoppable wave about to break, he ignored both the heavy hand on his shoulder and the tug on the cord, until it began to tighten around his throat. The wave crashed with a thunderous roar; his brief frisson of fear was lost in a great gasp of ecstasy, but immediately the cord was pulled so tight that he was unable to draw in a new breath.

"… find you …" whispered a voice, but it made no sense and anyway, Jude started to choke. His hands pawed ineffectually at his neck. He couldn't see his attacker. Neither could he cry out at the sudden agonising pain in his side; the internalised scream ricocheted round his skull as his searching fingers found first the hot, wet sticky warmth spreading out over his ribs and then the knife hilt. In the same moment someone – it could surely only have been Tyrod because all he could see was stars – delivered an almighty blow to the back of his head.

The stars went out.

The world turned black.

Jude found himself falling, just as in the very worst of his dreams, falling, falling for ever into a bottomless abyss.

# 8

Thankfully the abyss was *not* bottomless. Considering the speed at which he seemed to have been falling, and the amount of times he turned tip over arse whilst doing so, Jude was surprised when he landed on hard stone floor as lightly as if he'd been a snatch of thistledown. His first act was to ease the plaited cord from his neck and he was even more surprised to find that there was no pain. It was still pitch dark, but he could feel the bloody weal where the cord had dug deep into his flesh and he couldn't stop his head from lolling to one side. His skull felt a bit odd, too – touching it produced unpleasant grating sensations, but no pain there or in the gaping wound in his side. He sat and thought over all that had happened for a while, wondering how much of it had been part of the task. Was the journey with that final battle to get the wagon up the hill part of it? Was what had taken place in the tower between him and … and Kid, he supposed … also part of the task? And what was the point of it all?

He didn't understand. He had never understood.

Surely a hero should know what he was doing. It was too late now.

Then Jude remembered that Ersay had asked if he was ready to go in search of something lost, without telling him where to go or what to look for. And yet that, she'd said, was also the task. His thinking went round in circles, getting nowhere.

After a while, Jude stood up and reached into the darkness. He was in a narrow passage, the walls made of damp cold stone, slimy in places, and the ceiling hardly a hand span above his head, dank, and dripping ice cold water. He moved forward very cautiously, one step at a time, arms outstretched.

A tiny light appeared, so small that he thought it must be far distant. It was not: suddenly and without warning the way was blocked. Jude's groping hands found first solid timber then metal hinges and he realised the barricade was simply a huge door – a door moreover without any handle. He pushed gently and the door shifted a fraction. Jude let it close again and stood irresolute in the darkness knowing that since there was no going back, he had to go on, but fearful – anything could be on the other side. His heart set up an uncomfortable drum beat in response to that thought. The light source was a chink between two of the door's panels, too high up to be of any use, but when he put his ear against the wood, Jude could make out the muffled sounds of music ... and something else, a noise which rose and fell, unfamiliar but reminiscent of enraged bees swarming round a disturbed nest.

Screwing up his courage, Jude threw himself against the door. It swung open so easily that he fell forward into light of such intensity that he was temporarily blinded, into noise so loud that he could distinguish no individual sound, tumbled down a series of shallow steps and lay flat on his back, looking up at the door. As he'd surmised it was made of thick planks; these were studded with large-headed nails and set within a stone archway composed of three pointed arches, each carved inside the other, exactly like the one on the hollow tower.

Now Jude picked himself up and faced forward, shielding his eyes against the light. As they grew accustomed to its brilliance, he discovered he was in a hall so enormous that it was impossible to see either the sides or the far end. Lines of massive stone columns marched away into the distance and, looking up, he saw these supported a vaulted ceiling, from which hung metal contraptions, something like wheel rims, holding as many candles as there were – or at least, used to be – stars in the sky.

And now he realised what caused a noise loud enough to penetrate the door's great thickness. The hall was packed full of people, more people than he'd seen in his entire lifetime, more people than he could ever have imagined, all decked out in splendid finery, some dancing, some playing musical instruments, some standing in groups chatting, some playing board or ball games, a few pacing backwards and forwards apparently deep in thought, but most seated at immensely long tables – lit by yet more candles set only a hand's width apart – feasting and merrymaking, laughing and flirting, shouting to one another, picking mock squabbles, eating, eating, eating. Jude's eyes widened at the amount of food on the tables. This was the stuff of Osker's stories. Gold and silver platters – there was no space between the platters and the platters went on for ever – were heaped with meats and fruit and all sorts of other delicacies he didn't recognise but which were being guzzled as if there were no tomorrow.

Something crunched beneath his feet. Looking down, Jude saw that the cold, smooth floor was strewn with herbs, a few of which still clung to his blood-stained tunic. It comforted him that he recognised some of them – Meadow Maid, Woodruff, Withy-wind, Sweet-sop – all plants valued by Bett and Ma for their sweet smells, especially valuable in times of sickness, or death, and no sooner had the thought crossed his mind than he breathed in a great rush of their sappy green fragrance. He carefully brushed off the last of the leaves and stalks, sniffing the air in anticipation of the aroma of cooked meats and untried delicacies. For a long moment there was nothing, then, as he conjured up hopeful memories of gorging on clay-baked hedge-pig and roasted trow-fish, rabbit stews and the rare pleasure of badger meat, the air became thick and weighted with their savoury smells. His mouth began to water.

As yet, nobody seemed to have noticed his presence.

Supposing he'd better make himself known, Jude took two tentative steps forward. A bell rang. Everyone immediately stopped whatever they were doing and turned to face him. There was a long moment of silence and then a little light applause, after which the watchers appeared to lose interest and the noise rapidly built up to its previous level. It was hard to know what to do next. Jude surveyed the hall, looking for an empty chair where he might slide in quietly and partake of the feast. Before he could do so, he noticed a stout man, dressed in green, richly embroidered robes and wreathed in smiles, advancing down the central aisle.

"Welcome, young champion, welcome. I am Arown, your host, and you …?" he inclined his head.

"I'm Jude," said Jude, pushing his lolling head into an upright position.

"*Sir* Jude? *Lord* Jude?"

"No." Jude laughed, thinking the questions a joke. These were titles from fireside tales. "Just Jude."

"Ah." Arown grimaced. "Well, no matter. Times change and it's a long time since anyone came through that particular door."

"What happens now?" asked Jude. "Do I stay here?"

"You *can*," Arown said, with careful emphasis. "Yes, you're very welcome to stay here forever should you wish. Many do." He looked Jude up and down. "Come. Join us. Take some refreshment after your trials."

"Perhaps if I could wash first," Jude muttered, embarrassed by the comparison between his blood-stained rags and the fine garments of his host. The air quivered. He blinked. One moment he'd been filthy, dressed in a tattered tunic and trousers of coarsely woven stingweed cloth, the next he was clean and fresh and wearing soft green garments almost as fine as Arown's. "How …?"

But Arown only shrugged and beckoned Jude to follow him into the hall. All heads turned to watch them pass and there was a great deal of whispering behind hands, but Jude never caught one word of what was being said. He surreptitiously fingered the soft fabric of his new clothing, marvelling at its lightness. There were bands of intricate embroidery at the cuffs, circles and spirals for the most part, and it was while he was admiring the silver thread that Jude noticed every trace of the vile blackness had disappeared from his fore-arms. His hands flew to his neck, his skull, his side. His head was erect, all the wounds had gone; he was whole again. This was obviously a very good place to be. Jude would have liked to question Arown about such speedy healing, but his host seemed disinclined to talk, perhaps because of the uproar that increased in volume with every step they took. They walked for an exceedingly long time and it seemed to Jude that the further into the hall they went the more splendid the food became and the more extravagant the clothing.

Finally Arown dropped into a gilded chair and directed Jude to a slightly less ornate one at his right hand. Opposite him sat a man wrapped in a dark green cloak who acknowledged his arrival with a chilly nod. "Nudth," indicated Arown, "and these fair ladies are Blomweth, Ayf, and Arianrow."

Jude awkwardly muttered greetings. Nudth merely narrowed his eyes. The women, all of whom were dressed in the deepest darkest midnight blue with silver girdle-chains and necklaces hung with tiny moons in all their phases – crescent, gibbous, full – gracefully inclined their heads and immediately looked elsewhere.

"Sit down. Sit down. Some wine … or perhaps you'd prefer ale?" Never having tasted either, Jude simply nodded. Arown passed him a brimming goblet. "Try that. I warrant you'll never have tasted finer."

"Thank you." Jude took a cautious sip and nodded polite appreciation, though to him it tasted like slightly muddy spring water.

Arown raised his own goblet. "To the champion," he roared and every head turned towards Jude and every goblet was raised as they echoed Arown's words.

"And now," said Arown, "the champion must eat." He gestured up and down the table. "Choose what you will. Everything the stomach of man desires is here. Allow me to serve you."

He picked up a knife and waited expectantly while Jude inspected the platters. As far as he could see, the majority held roast birds, big and small, plucked clean of every last feather but with their heads still on. Their eyes were flat and dull; their beaks drooped. A few had been boned and submerged in variously coloured sauces. On one platter sat a very large bird, its body cavity stuffed with a smaller bird that had itself been stuffed with an even smaller one, and on seemingly *ad infinitum*. Jude's stomach turned.

"Birds – don't they make you sick?"

Arown smiled. "There can be no illness here."

A woman passed behind them. She wore a heavily beaded scarlet dress slashed to the navel and with sleeves so long that they trailed along the floor. She leaned over Jude and her thick black hair enclosed them in a curtain, shutting them off from their surroundings, reminding him of other hair and another place. "Have a plum," she breathed. "Try a peach. Try me."

"Uh, uh ... no thanks." Jude fought free of the hair, trying not to stare at the woman's breasts. She hovered for a moment and then flounced away.

"There will be many such offers," said Arown. He raised an eyebrow and nodded at the table. "Well?"

"I can't eat bird," said Jude. "Where I come from birds bring sickness and death."

"You'd enjoy something more exotic, perhaps." Arown clapped his hands and two particularly massive platters were passed along the table. One supported an ugly white-feathered creature with an astonishingly long neck and a small head, the other an equally hideous blue and green monstrosity with a huge fan tail.

Jude eyed them doubtfully. "Ain't they birds, too?"

"Good gracious, no." Arown looked deeply affronted. "The silver platter bears a swan, the other a peacock. Both are the food of kings and the rightful reward of the champion. I suggest you try the swan."

A tiny gold crown adorned the white creature's head and there was a garland of yellow kingcup flowers around its neck. Obviously this was something special, nevertheless it was still covered in feathers, it had a beak, it had outspread wings, and it had big flat orange feet with claws. Bluddy thing was a bird, no doubt about it. And yet, that long neck looked more like snake. Peering at it closely, Jude discovered that the wings and feathers were a kind of decorative blanket supported on a frame. Maybe what lay underneath was really some sort of snake, or even several snakes, carefully arranged and disguised as a bird. They'd eaten snake once or twice, but why bother now? As for the other one … Jude caught Arown's glare. Clearly examining things at very close range disturbed his host. He stopped.

"There is chawdron to accompany the swan." Arown passed a bowl of something to Jude who sniffed cautiously at what looked like finely chopped guts in black goo. The stuff reminded him of his discoloured limbs on the green hill. He declined.

Arown looked most put out. "Some fish then? Salmon? Carp? Or perhaps Pike with galentyne sauce. Delicious, I assure you."

Jude looked about him and saw a whole pig with its jaws clamped on an apple. He'd once tasted pig, long ago, when several travelling groups had come together for some festivity or other. He remembered the huge fire pit, the smell of roasting flesh, the sizzling fat that made the throat gag and the eyes stream. The memory conjured up another image – of trees and snow and screaming – that flashed across his mind and was gone, leaving only inexplicable sadness. Jude numbly indicated his choice.

"Ah, the boar – food of the warrior," said Arown, and laughed. He carved a generous plateful and ripped off a swan's leg for himself. Jude saw that the big flat bird feet were not attached. The creature was undoubtedly disguised snake.

He tasted the boar's meat. It was pleasant enough but what he really fancied was the simple comforting food of the old days; jessnuts, for example. Jude blinked as a bowlful immediately materialised at his elbow, newly roasted, and still so hot that he had to toss them from hand to hand before they were cool enough to peel. Suddenly ravenous, he crammed them into his mouth, one after the other. But there was a curious thing, the first half dozen were delicious, every bit as good as he remembered, after that the taste diminished rapidly until it was little better than eating wood flakes as in hungry times, or even ashes, which had been an early mistake. Since Arown seemed preoccupied with his swan's leg, Jude tried a few experiments, wishing for bowls of raspberries, strawberries, fat pipberries and goose-gogs. Each time they appeared immediately and tasted sweet as greedy handfuls fresh-gathered at the edge of a wood with the sun still on them, and almost as good as those Ersay had given them early in their journey together. It was highly satisfactory – as long as he ate only a few. After that the taste soon palled and once again he might as well have been chewing on wood shavings.

Busy with his experiments, Jude turned clumsy and knocked a knife from the table. He bent to retrieve it, taking the opportunity to ascertain that his legs were as free of the blackness as his arms.

A movement beneath the strewn herbs caught his eye. Clearing a space with his feet, he saw that the floor was made of glass: he could see straight through it. Immediately below were upturned faces distorted by howling, weeping and screaming, giving the appearance of being in the throes of extreme agony. Alarmed, Jude pushed back his chair. He grabbed the sleeve of the man sitting opposite who sat with his arms folded, eating nothing and watching everything and, unable to remember his name, blurted: "What's up with these people beneath us?"

The fellow coughed. "I didn't catch your name."

"Jude. I'm Jude." He glanced down and saw a woman tearing her hair out in handfuls. Her mouth was stretched open as if in a great howl of despair. Her face was almost purple. "What's happening to them? Can they see us?"

"I believe you were told that my name is Nudth." He sighed heavily, waiting until Jude remembered his manners, apologised, and mumbled the simple courtesies he'd learned from Ma before continuing. "Those are the people who believe in eternal damnation for having made mistakes. They imagine themselves being eaten alive, burned or flayed, or whatever other painful and demeaning punishments their imaginations can devise. Like so much else, it is an illusion. Ignore them. And, no, for the most part they can't see us."

Jude jumped as a great gobbet of blood hit the other side of the floor. It looked real enough. He swallowed hard. "And if they can? What do you do then?"

"Do?" Nudth looked surprised. "We bring them to join us. It means the madness has passed and they've once more become aware of the natural order of things."

"Oh." Jude drew his chair back into place and forced himself not to keep watching.

"You'll find a garden over there," Nudth gestured vaguely to the opposite side of the hall, "with hundreds of thousands of others, all identically dressed in white robes and wearing wings. All the poor things want to do is to walk on the grass, smile serenely, and listen to harps being played. Think how tedious that must get. And right next to it, another place, one of tranquil orchards and shaded courtyards with fountains, where men go in pursuit of the illusion of four and twenty perpetual virgins." He shook his head. "There are many more: all variations on a theme. The beliefs fostered in the Otherworld are sometimes past all understanding, but leave them long enough and they all see sense in the end."

"Oh." Jude thought for a moment. "What's the Otherworld?"

Nudth did a double take. One eyebrow shot up. "The place you came from, of course."

"And where is this?"

"To them, this is also known as the Otherworld, though some prefer to call it the Underworld."

Jude looked down at himself. He surreptitiously pinched his leg. The sensation was curious, not painful, not really a feeling, more the memory of feeling. "Am I dead then?"

Nudth hesitated, as though choosing his words carefully. "It may be that you are simply passing through."

"And does everybody come here?" persisted Jude, thinking of Ma, Bett and the others. He tried to hang on to the thought, scanning the faces of the milling crowds, but it melted and was quickly forgotten.

Nudth nodded matter-of-factly. "Try some venison," he suggested.

"No thanks."

"Mmm, not as popular as it was: odd. How about a little mutton? Pottage? Some cheese, perhaps?"

"Why does everybody keep going on about food?" protested Jude. "It ain't stopped since I got here. Eat this. Eat that. Try these. Taste the other. I ain't forever hungry."

"Really?" Nudth looked surprised. "Here we help you settle in by satisfying all your strongest desires whilst living in the Otherworld. Apparently yours was food. Oh, and comfort: fires, warm blankets, and soft beds. Those also seem to have been important to you." His forehead creased as he stared intently at Jude. "And women, perhaps? Oh, yes, we read your secret desires. We weigh you up on arrival. Nothing usually gets past us."

Several beautiful young women in low cut gowns chose that moment to sashay by, peeping and giggling. Jude looked away. They were not Ersay. Neither were any of them Kid, and that was probably more important.

"Ah," said Nudth, though Jude had not uttered a word. He pushed away his unused platter. "Tell us stories of your adventures in the Otherworld."

A small crowd gathered and Jude stumblingly launched into an account of the trials, tribulations and small pleasures of life in the wagon. For the most part his audience listened politely enough, though stifling yawns from time to time. The loss of his group engendered a little interest, as did the appearance of Ersay, but it was the discovery of the captive Kid that really caught their attention.

A woman leaned forward, twisting her hands. "Yes, go on, go on. Did you rescue the dishonoured maiden?"

"Was she beautiful?" demanded another.

"Yes," Jude said, wistfully, knowing now that it was true. "Yes, she is beautiful." He described, with some flagrant exaggeration, the freeing of Kid and the escape with her enraged captors in hot pursuit.

"Did you not stop and challenge them to combat?" demanded a stout fellow dressed in darkest red. "Did you not strike their loathsome heads from their foul bodies? Did you not split them from skull pan to testicles?"

"There were too many," Jude said, weakly, "and we were too few." He moved on to a description of the holes in the land. The yawns grew more pronounced. His description of the attack by the dog-pack met with sneers and theatrical incredulity from the fellow in red.

"How many dogs did you say?"

Jude stood his ground. "Lots: two score or more."

The other's lip curled. He snapped his fingers and a huge pack of white dogs, all with red ears, some spotted with red, some striped, streamed through the hall, unstoppable as a flood-swollen river in full spate, baying loudly, the noise gradually fading into the sound of winter storms rushing through a great forest as they disappeared into the far distance. His nostrils flared. "Were the dogs as many as those?"

Jude shook his head.

"Then did you run them through? Did you spit them upon your sword?" And when Jude didn't answer, the man in red cried: "No more! This is peasant stuff. Give us your tales of knightly combat."

"I have none," Jude said in a flat voice, and his audience lost interest and drifted away.

The man sitting on his right side nudged him in the ribs. "Take no notice of them, son. They only wants to hear about bluddy tom-fool tournaments and kerchief waving and play-battles. There's nothing wrong with peasants. Peasants is the dung what the feasting at the lords' tables depends on." He sniffed and wiped his nose with the back of his hand. "I was in your boots once, son. In my time I was the big sacrifice of the year. Done the rite, then got strangled, knocked on the head, stuck like a pig and pushed into a bog to rot, that's me. Nice."

Jude noticed that his face and hair were covered in grease. Meat juices had trickled down his chin to lodge amongst his bristly stubble and in the folds of his neck. Even his ear lobes shone. But he also had red hair, albeit thin and stringy. Jude asked him about it. The fellow puffed out his chest. "Special, ain't we, being neither dark nor fair, not one nor the other, and yet both. Not many of us about, son. It's all part of the 'in-between' thing – day and night, water and land, dark and light. They explained it all to me once: point of change or something. That stuff. " A tinge of resentment crept into his voice. "Tol, that's me. I was the last champion here till you come along. That's my seat what you're sitting on."

"Sorry."

"You ain't to blame, son." Tol visibly brightened. "Fact is, I shouldn't have been sat there for so long, but nobody came and nobody came. These here," he jerked his head towards a line of men further down the table, "they be the ones what come just before me. One a year, usually, more if times turned extra bad. They all come the same way – first the rite, then the strangling, then their heads bashed in, then a stick poked through their guts, and then chucked into the bog. All done proper mind, all done for The Lady, *all in a good cause.* But when nobody came and nobody came, we said to ourselves, we said, whole bluddy lot must have gone to rat shit after they done us."

"I see," said Jude. "Tol, about that rite …"

"Huh-huh-huh!" Tol laughed so hard that he snorted one end and farted the other. He slapped Jude's thigh several times. "Almost made it worthwhile, didn't it, son? Ooh ah, yes, even with that muck they made us eat first. Reckon we'd go through it all again for a bit more of that." He seized some small roast bird, ripped off the breast meat and shovelled the whole lot into his mouth.

Jude averted his eyes and waited until the worst of the noise had died down before asking: "And the task? Did you finish the task?"

"O," spluttered Tol while chewing vigorously. "I-bova?"

"So you're saying you didn't finish it?" asked Jude, confused. "Why?"

"Why?" Tol gave his fingers a perfunctory licking before wiping them the full length of his tunic. "Why? It's bluddy all right here, that's why, so like I said, why bother? Never run short of nothing in this place. Never. You can eat yourself silly, and then some. I ain't stopped since I got here. Thing is, son, living like this is what I was done in for back home. See what I mean? All they wanted was for every day to be as full of plenty as this. You want my advice – stay here. You won't ever want for nothing. Get bored and there's outside, gardens and that, trees all weighed down with fruit like you've never seen. Or you can go hunting. Dogs. Horses. Spears. Anything you want. Hunt all day and all night if you feel like it. No shortage of game. And," he lowered his voice, "there ain't no shortage of willing women, neither." He grinned horribly, showing brown teeth stuck with morsels of meat. "No, son, that's me done. Far as I'm concerned I've been through enough."

"But what about Ersay?"

"Er-who?" Tol stared, mouth still hanging open. "Oh, you mean The Lady. Well, reckon I done my bit getting strangled, knocked on the head, stuck like a pig and pushed into a bog to rot. There weren't much more to it, son."

"There was," Jude, said impatiently. "What about taking back whatever it was that was lost?"

"Dunno." Tol prised the apple out of the boar's mouth, sniffed at it, took a bite and threw the rest over his shoulder. His stubby fingers dug into the boar's fat cheek. He strained to tear off the flesh. "Never knew or can't remember. What I do know is I ain't shifting from here for nothing nor nobody." He triumphantly held aloft two dripping handfuls of meat. "Want some?" Jude looked from him to the exposed yellow tusks of the boar. He shook his head. Tol shrugged. "Please yourself, son – all the more for me." Opening his mouth as wide as possible, he began ramming in the first fistful of meat.

Jude turned away from what was rapidly becoming a loathsome spectacle to find both Nudth and Arown regarding him intently. The three women in midnight blue – he couldn't remember their names – were also watching him. One sat on each side of Nudth, the third stood behind him, her hands on his shoulders. They listened in silence, slowly telling the little silver moons on their jewellery, their movements synchronised, their faces beautiful but stern.

"So, Jude," said Arown, his tone solemn, "would you stay and become like Tol? Or will you shoulder your task and continue on your way?"

"I promised myself I'd finish what I started," Jude looked down and began playing with the cuff of his tunic, "but …"

"Stay," suggested Nudth. "To go forward may be dangerous. Who knows what lies ahead?"

Arown leaned forward. "And yet a promise is a promise."

"Yes, I know." Jude nodded vigorously, without looking up.

"But, like Tol, you've already done so much," declared Nudth, drumming his fingers against the table. "Why not let someone else take it on?"

"*Is* there anyone else?" enquired the woman to the left of Nudth.

"No, there ain't," said Jude and looked her full in the face. Something about her reminded him of Ersay, for all that she was dark and Ersay so fair, but he couldn't work out what it was. "Leastways I don't think so. And it ain't that I don't want to do it, even though I am scared, but …"

"There was a time," put in Arown, "when you told yourself you would do anything for this Ersay, anything, lay down your life if necessary."

"And so he did," murmured Nudth. "This Ersay is undoubtedly a harsh mistress." There followed a long pause throughout which he continued to watch Jude intently. Jude fidgeted under his scrutiny. He thought of Ersay's beauty and her generosity. Then he remembered her treatment of the men who'd threatened her on the road.

"Yes," he said, doubtfully. "She can be, but …"

Somewhere a bell rang with a high, silvery tone, not at all like the one which had announced his arrival. The hall fell silent. Jude was suddenly aware of many eyes watching him. Although he kept his own eyes fixed on Nudth, he got the impression that people were standing up and moving closer.

"Once!" declared Arown.

"And it's true to say that Ersay made life very difficult for you," continued Nudth, leaning his chin on his steepled fingers.

Jude frowned. He supposed at times she had, what with pulling the wagon round that narrow path and so on. Not to mention the disappearing when they needed her most. "Yeh," he agreed, reluctantly, "but –" And looked up, startled, as the high-toned bell rang again, nearer this time, almost directly overhead.

"Twice!" said Arown and a host of onlookers softly repeated the word, so that it sounded as if echoes of his utterance were ricocheting round the hall.

"Twice what?" Jude asked. He looked from Nudth to Arown, and then at the women. All their faces were expressionless; nobody answered so he ploughed on regardless. "What I was trying to say was … but only because Ersay won't say what it is she wants. And if I'm still doing the task I don't know how to finish it."

Arown leaned back in his chair. "How much do you know?"

"Ersay told me to bring back what has been lost. I don't know what it is or where to find it."

"Oh that nonsense again," said Nudth, sardonically. "Yes, yes, the so-called vessel beyond price. At the end of every age there is some container – bowl, cooking pot, chamber pot, cauldron, chalice, cup, call it what you will – that needs taking back to the Otherworld. Then the land will fruit and flower again, the creatures proliferate, the population increase and so on and so on – slippery slope, young man, slippery slope. It will all come to a bad end. It always does. Not a worthwhile venture. Not worth risking your skin over. Why not stay here and enjoy yourself." Nudth paused. "She asks too much," he murmured. There was a note of expectancy in the statement. It was now very quiet in the hall, even though a quick glance showed Jude that even more people had crowded round to listen.

"She asks too much," repeated Nudth, a trifle louder.

Jude struggled to get his thoughts in order. He still was no wiser about the task. He only knew what seemed right so that was what he'd do. Anyway, his spirits lightened at the thought, if the pot or whatever and where ever it was, had to be taken *back* to Ersay and if she still cared for and protected Kid, then maybe there was a chance of finding the girl again.

"SHE ASKS TOO MUCH," roared Nudth, and this time his words really did echo round the hall.

"No," retorted Jude, springing to his feet, "she does not. And whatever she wants me to do I will do to the best of my ability, even if I fail trying."

Someone laughed, but not unkindly. A murmur that might have been approval ran through the crowd.

"Ah," said Nudth and his whole demeanour changed. He smiled. "Go then, Jude. May your pointless trials and tribulations be immortalised in story and song – like all the other doomed champions who have passed this way."

"Doomed?" asked Jude.

"There's only one path for all of us so whatever your striving, even if you do succeed, even if you find your way out, you will walk this way again soon enough."

Jude nodded. He *thought* he understood.

"It's all part of the great cycle," Arown said, kindly, "in which, Jude, you play an important part."

Heartened, Jude appealed to Arown. "Doesn't anybody know what this container thing looks like?" Arown spread his hands and it was one of the women, Blomweth, he thought, who spoke.

"Appearance isn't a fixed thing, Jude. The vessel beyond price may take the form of a gem-encrusted golden goblet or a fire-blackened iron cooking pot, perhaps a clay bowl chipped from long use, a bull's horn, even a crude wooden beaker. The important thing is that it speaks *to you* of love, compassion and nurturing – all the worthwhile virtues." She smiled. "You will know it when you see it."

"That's what Ersay said," Jude tried to keep the despair out his voice. "And where must I go to find it?"

"Go to the far end of the hall," Nudth said, briskly. "There you will see several doors. You can't mistake yours – it's ornamented with a pair of fighting dragons." He peered from under his eyebrows. "How do you feel about confronting a dragon, young champion?"

"Only a b-big lizard-thing, ain't it?" Jude said uncertainly. Years ago Tattow had terrified him with tales of dragons, ellypunts and hippomusses until Ma had caught him at it and explained that these were only over-large lizards, tall pigs with long noses, and fat, squat horses. She'd emphasised her superior knowledge, he remembered, with a right hook to Tattow's jaw. "A very b-big lizard with w-wings."

Arown laughed. The women smiled.

"Quite big," Nudth agreed, drily. "But how about confronting two?"

Jude simply stared at him.

Nudth laughed. "Go through the door or not, as you choose." He turned away and reached for a wine flagon.

"But how will I ..." began Jude.

Nudth glanced over his shoulder. "Work it out for yourself. You do this alone, or not at all."

On and on Jude trudged. People stopped their feasting and stood up to watch him pass. A few shouted encouragement and some offered him food or drink. The noise rose and fell. Sometimes Jude thought he heard familiar voices and he scanned the faces in hope of seeing Ma or the others but through it all he kept walking. Eventually he saw an end wall in the distance and, after another interminable march, made out a row of dark openings that must be doors, only one of which was decorated. Jude altered his course slightly and plodded towards it.

A long and weary walk later, the door seemed as far away as ever and Jude became so tired that he stopped and sat cross-legged on the floor. He had no intention of falling asleep but his eyelids grew heavy and his head fell forward. When he woke, it was to utter confusion because in that first blink after wakening, sleepily squinting sideways, and from under his lids, Jude saw things as they really were.

The magnificent hall was only a dingy cavern dimly lit by spluttering torches and feeble rush lights stuck into the rock and its majestic pillars were stalactites growing slowly down to meet ancient stalagmites. Ferns grew in crevices. Water trickled down the slimy green walls. A thick layer of rotting ferns lay heaped on the floor, under which forms squirmed and gyrated beneath occasional skims of dirty ice. The men and women seated at the tables were grotesque, gaunt and old past all knowing, with sallow grey skin and red-rimmed sunken eyes, their pates bald or covered with sparse and wispy hair. Those men who had before appeared elegant, even dandified, were now revealed as vile creatures with bandy legs and sagging bellies, their skins covered with warty growths, and the beautiful women as ancient hags with pendulous breasts and humped backs. Most feet were bare and dirty, with long yellow curling nails. Their voices rose, thin and querulous; the noise that filled the great space was produced by countless bats hanging from the roof like a thick black crust or skimming the heads of the revellers. And the tables themselves were nothing more than rough hewn planks; the chairs uprooted tree stumps, the platters flat stones or large leaves. On the platters lay short lengths of water-logged wood or lumps of red clay moulded into diverse shapes. As Jude had suspected, both the wine and ale were plain water and none too fresh at that.

Jude began to wonder if there was anything else he hadn't seen properly. 'Like so much else, it is an illusion', Nudth said when speaking of the tormented people under the glass. Jude's mind fleetingly struggled with the concept as he wondered about the holes in the earth ... and then about the earth itself.

At least while he slept the door seemed to have come closer. He could see now that it was indeed ornamented with the images of two fearsome dragons – one red-gold and the other silvery-white, their open jaws ferociously clamped on each other's tails – so skilfully forged that they seemed to writhe and twist before his eyes. Once again this door was set within a triple arch. And once again it was reached by way of three shallow steps.

Jude closed the remaining distance in a few strides, pausing at the bottom of the steps when he noticed the dragons' round gem-stone eyes flickering as though watching his every movement. Wise eyes, he thought, and old, but not particularly kind. The old terrors returned: anything could happen behind that door. He fought to conquer his fear, but it was persuasive: he didn't have to go on, its soft whisper suggested; it wasn't too late to change his mind, to stay here and live at ease for ever. Jude gritted his teeth. Stay and he would become one of them, those that hung between the two worlds, neither dead nor alive. Besides, what would happen to Ersay if he didn't complete his task? And then there was Kid.

He forced himself to mount the steps.

As Jude turned the great metal handle with both hands, something alerted him and he glanced back. Arown, Nudth, the three women – Blomweth, Ayf and Arianrow – plus a handful of others stood facing him a few paces beyond the steps. Even they looked different – not decrepit like the guzzling carousing hordes at the tables, but taller, and very pale, with long braided hair that might have been spun from moonlight and eyes the colour of icy winter rain. All were dressed in misty grey robes that made them almost invisible when viewed from certain angles. Each of them exuded power, especially the women, and Jude realised now that this was what had reminded him so strongly of Ersay.

Arown took a step forward. "You chose wisely, Jude. You battled with your fears and won. May it go well with you until we meet again, and may that be later rather than sooner."

Jude raised one hand in farewell and pushed open the door, noticing as he slipped through, that he was once more wearing his tattered and blood-stained clothes.

## 9

The door slammed shut with a resounding boom before Jude had a chance to see what lay ahead, and he was back in pitch black darkness again. There was something malevolent about the quality of this particular darkness: the entire weight of whatever lay above seemed to press down on him. Jude thought of bodies buried deep within the earth and gritted his teeth.

From the way the noise was contained – there'd been no dying echoes – Jude guessed correctly that he was in a small space and hadn't taken more than ten cautious paces forward before his way was blocked by a second door. This one proved far more difficult to open. The great ring of a handle, so cold that his skin stuck to the metal, turned reluctantly with a great deal of teeth-jarring scraping and grating; even then the door opened little more than a couple of hand spans before jamming against the stone and started to close again as he strained to ease himself through the gap, spitefully catching the tail of his tunic just when he thought he'd made it. Jude tore himself free. Another few paces and he came to a third door, but this one was ajar, allowing him to slip through.

He was in another unlit passage. At first it felt much like the passage leading into the great hall, but whereas the walls in that passage had been dank and slippery, these were dry with a lumpy surface which he was loathe to touch even when he stumbled and almost fell over something – a collection of brittle sticks, perhaps, and a broken bowl – lying sprawled over the entire width of the passage. The floor beneath him was dry too, thick with dust, and striated as if coarse parallel lines had been gouged from the stone.

It was very quiet. All Jude could hear was the sound of his own breathing, the shuffle of his feet through the dust of ages, the occasional rasp of his tunic catching on the wall's protrusions. After a time a dim light, still a shade darker than twilight, seeped into the passage and since the further he went, the stronger it grew, Jude increased his pace until it was bright enough to let him see there were now passages branching off on either side of the main one, and that some of those appeared to branch again, and then again. It seemed wiser to keep going straight on.

Jude stopped abruptly as a howl of despair broke the stillness. "Who's there?" he called, attempting to keep the shameful quiver out of his voice. No answer came, but a bad smell wafted across his face, sweet and rotten, as if something had crawled in here to die.

And then the whispers began.

At first Jude was convinced that he wasn't alone; then he began to pick out voices from long ago, voices which he could no longer put a name or a face to but were familiar. And soon Ma's, Da's, Osker's, Bett's, even his own joined in. The voices were always in front of him. They rose and fell, ebbed and flowed, like distant music played on one of Tattow's less successful elderwood pipes, but however quickly Jude hurried towards the sound, he never managed to catch more than a few disjointed words.

The light was stronger now. This was a mixed blessing since it meant Jude discovered that the walls were macabre hurdles formed of an uncountable number of bones packed within staves, and topped with human skulls, many horribly smashed, holed or cleaved. He recoiled from the sight, stumbling against the opposite wall which grated and crunched and spilled broken splinters of bone, vertebrae and phalanges onto floor that he could now see was entirely composed of closely packed thigh bones. Moving on fast, Jude tried to lift his feet as he walked rather than scuffing through dust left by time's slow grinding down of these ghastly relics.

Even that wasn't so bad, at least not compared with what lay head. A few paces in front of him the passage forked. He'd resolved to keep going straight ahead, now it was impossible. Since there was nothing to choose between the two, Jude took the left hand passage. It immediately forked again. He beat a hurried retreat and tried the right, which continued for twenty paces or so before turning a corner where it ended abruptly. A row of skulls, their gap-toothed jaws set in cheerful grins, peered down at him and Jude fled in dismay from the silent mocking laughter of the dead. Unwillingly, and with dragging feet, he returned to the left hand passage. The whispers followed him.

It took him a while to realise he was trapped within a labyrinth.

Many and terrible had been Bett's tales of the plights of heroes in ancient labyrinths; as he recalled there was always something large and hideous to do bloody battle with at its heart. Resigned to the prospect of another nasty end Jude trudged on, turning this way, that way, whenever possible keeping straight on, but with no other plan, until he was convinced – surely he'd seen that jaw bone with teeth protruding at impossible angles before, and already passed this thigh bone almost as tall as his entire body, besides look at how the dust had been scuffed by many trails of footprints – that he was walking in circles.

Jude bent and drew a large cross in the dust before setting off again. A short while later the passage divided into three. The central fork was blocked a few paces in; retracing his steps, he tried to decide between the left- and the right-hand fork, only to find that both of them were now marked with a large cross. Jude looked behind him. No one was there. Neither was there any sound of other footfalls, though the whispers had crept closer. He walked backwards looking for his original cross but must have missed the turning. Determined not to panic, Jude drew a large circle around the left-hand cross and started off again. Every passage he came to thereafter was marked by a cross within a circle. He began to run, faster, faster still, but only came to another dead end; whirling round he was confronted by another where a moment there'd before been clear passageway.

With a great howl of despair, Jude fell to his knees ... and recognised the sound. It was the cry he'd heard just before he entered the labyrinth. And since time was so tangled here, he supposed morosely that it was him rotting and creating the vile smell, too. There seemed no point in plodding on when the end was inevitable and anyway, he was sick and tired of walking. Deep gloom settled onto his shoulders, sending his spirits plummeting still further. The whispers ceased abruptly as Jude rolled himself into a tight ball, keeping well clear of the walls, and waited. One thing was sure: he would rather have died at the edge of a wood than here, or in a ditch by the highway, or better still, ended it on the hilltop with Kid beside him.

But it was when Jude began to visualise Kid perched up on the box or running alongside the wagon, her black hair gleaming, her brown skin glowing, her eyes flashing while she teased and taunted him, that his visions came back to haunt him as fleeting glimpses of the square, the forest clearing, the ruined land.

According to Tyrod mankind had done nothing to honour the earth, from the very start they'd only taken, taken, and then taken some more so – Jude being the scapegoat – it was reasonable to suppose the irascible old man had always been responsible for plunging him into those other places, other times.

Was it true? Not being able to see the bigger picture, Jude couldn't tell. He only knew what happened in his own little group and on their behalf Jude resented the accusation. They'd done the right things, chanted the proper words and asked for both guidance and blessings at each crossroads. The turning of the year had been marked without fail, the changing of the seasons always celebrated. Every one of them had been very careful to leave no mark of their passing on the land.

And yet … Jude shifted uncomfortably. And yet there was … no denying their avariciousness. When Da was alive he cared nothing for other people's rights of ownership; he took whatever he could find, no matter who it belonged to, even if he had no immediate use for the thing, even if it left others in desperate need. Ma and Bett and the others snatched up everything, stripped trees and bushes bare, picked up every last grain of wheat, dug patches of earth over and over again to find a single missed root, however small, however wizened, without a care for those that might come after them. They did it out of long engrained habit, even when times weren't hard, but this was survival, tomorrow there might be nothing at all. What else could they have done?

Another wave of stench hit him full in the face and Jude covered his nose.

Life was hard. Ma and the others were always afraid of not having enough because they'd known times of real hunger. That was how it was for mankind; always had been as far as Jude knew. Where he'd just been – in the hall of Arown and Nudth – was the only place he'd ever seen freedom from want and that had been illusory. Jude thought he would like to tax Tyrod with this, if only he could find the way back. He got to his feet and, shuddering, brushed off the soft grey bone-dust. It occurred to him that towards the end of the journey up the hill, his eyes blinded by sweat and exhaustion, he'd been forced to rely on his feet to keep to the seven fold path. It was worth a try.

Jude closed his eyes and stepped forward into the unknown, even keeping his arms down by his sides, until he could stand it no more. When he opened them he was standing in a well-lit passage that widened at the far end, opening out into a hollow chamber, like a cave, its roof and walls a mass of tightly interlaced roots that had fingered through the rocks and held on tight. The roots themselves had a purplish-grey tinge that reminded him of the gnarled veins in Bett's skinny legs and the low background drone, almost but not quite a growl, permeating the space could almost have been her subdued grumbling at the end of a long day's trek. The light source was a ragged hole, high above, through which drifted a ribbon of faint mist or smoke, but Jude saw that the spreading roots below it formed a rough natural ladder that would be easy enough to climb.

The chamber was full of life. Large black beetles, which Jude knew from experience were no good for eating, scurried across the floor, carrying off small fragments of greyish-brown matter that continually filtered down through the roots above his head. Jude had his suspicions about these – the stink being so much stronger here that it was hard not to retch – but having no wish to enquire into their precise nature, he quickly averted his eyes. The mice were more of a problem, emerging from countless nooks and crannies amongst the stones to pour down the walls like foaming flood water. These were tiny with meagre white fur that hardly covered their pink skin, bright red eyes, and none of the usual rodent shyness: they swirled round his feet and climbed up his legs. Jude beat them off but they came back for more; a few even nosed inside his trousers, pulling at the frayed fabric and carrying off long threads before getting even bolder and yanking at his leg hair with strong little teeth.

The background drone suddenly soared and the accompanying blast of wind carried a cloud of thick white warm mist through the hole, swirling round the chamber to blot out everything but the brighter circle of light high above. There was no mistaking the noise now, it was certainly furious growling and not from a single throat either. This must be the heart of the maze: above him were the two dragons. Jude wanted to linger a while, savouring the place's relative safety, bracing himself for whatever came next, but the mice began swarming up his legs, inside his trousers as well as outside. A few reached his shoulders and began burrowing into his hair, and the feel of their small claws and whippy tails, never mind the nips, pulls and bites, was more than he could bear. Shaking them off, he ran blindly towards the mist-shrouded wall and began to haul his tired body hand-over-hand up the rungs of the root ladder.

Jude emerged into a cold place choked with even denser mist and his heart thumped as he crouched low, making himself small while he waited for it to clear.

First he saw the pit. And then he smelled the full force of its stench. Little by little the mist retreated revealing a huge stone platform encircling the trunk of a very large, very ancient tree. The tree appeared to be dead. The pit was actually a wide ditch, something like a moat and perhaps three times his height across, surrounding the platform, and it was full of weapons: countless swords, knives, spears, axes, cudgels and bows, even a catapult or two. Full of bodies too, spent heroes, a few in rusty armour, but all in various states of decay; it was the dragons rolling and threshing their wings on the inner platform that sent fragments of rotting flesh raining down into the cavern below.

Jude could hardly bring himself to look at the dragons. To say that they were big lizards was something of an understatement. No wonder Arown had laughed. He tried to comfort himself by thinking of them as being like gentle Fareed, only bigger, a lot bigger. Any horse was potentially dangerous, its huge feet could kill with a single blow, the great teeth were capable of taking a hefty bite out of more or less anything, but they usually weren't. It didn't work. The dragons were vast: almost as tall as the wagon at their shoulders and longer from snout to tail-tip than the wagon with Fareed harnessed in front of it and neither looked as if being gentle formed any part of their make up. Both had their eyes closed and he supposed they slept, but after a few moments rest they resumed their struggles, rearing and bucking and twisting their heads, their hot breath turning into steam as it collided with the chilly atmosphere, their vast wings churning the coiling boiling clouds of mist and stirring the decomposing bodies in the ditch. Above them, the tree trembled and shook, its limbs screaking as they rubbed against each other, its long black twiggy fingers scraping helplessly at the air. The noise peaked and the dragons collapsed again.

Cupping his hand over his nose, Jude crept closer and squinted at the tree through the swirling mist. Though tall, it was hunched and bent as an old, old woman, its trunk so knobbled and knotted, the bark so deeply grooved, that countless lopsided and wrinkled faces seemed to be staring back. But that wasn't what interested him. He could see now what the dragons were guarding. Wedged into every nook and cranny, every hollow and fissure, and balanced on every knobbed elbow was a huge variety of vessels, some intensely beautiful, some purely practical, and a great many that managed to be both. Jude examined them as best he could through the thinning rags of mist, wondering which one would best please Ersay. His gaze flitted between a whole array of gleaming chalices, two- sometimes three-handled and set with sparkling gems, and on to an exquisite green glass goblet with a swirled stem slender as a flower stalk, past it to diverse receptacles of gold, silver or exquisitely carved tusk and bone, to cups, porringers, mortars, and came to rest on a huge black iron cooking pot that Ma would have given her eye teeth for.

And then, right at the top of the tree, wedged between two up-thrusting bare branches, Jude saw the bowl that should have burned on Osker's funeral pyre. How it came to be here he couldn't tell. He supposed by rights that his own body should now be mouldering in the tower – if any of it still existed – but then, time did not run as it should here, it slipped backwards and sideways and, for all he knew, leaped forwards as well. Jude took a few paces in the tree's direction, longing to hold the bowl, if only for a moment: it was all that remained of a past which seemed sunny and golden in retrospect. He hurriedly jumped back again as the dragons resumed their eternal battle, hardly knowing whether to cover his nose against the smell or his ears against the din.

After watching for a while, Jude realised that they were not fighting at all, simply engaged in a desperate struggle to get free. He could see now that both dragons had simple iron muzzles secured around their jaws, locking them shut and thereby forcing each to keep its grip on the other's tail. It occurred to him that many a fine fireside tale of bloody battle and great cunning could be spun from a little skilful disregard of this fact, but this presupposed a great many things: getting out of here, a fire, some ground to put it on, and listeners. At any rate, he was safe enough as long as he stayed out of reach of those terrible wings – though standing at a distance wouldn't get him the bowl. Jude saw too that all was not right with the dragons: many of the white dragon's silver scales had become dull and leaden whilst those of the red-gold dragon were tarnished mud-brown and black. There were a few small nicks and scars on their underbellies, presumably inflicted by those now languishing in the ditch, but he looked in vain for other signs of weakness.

Others had come this way and tried to kill the dragons. Some had been armed and protected. Even so, they hadn't stood a chance – the contents of the ditch were evidence of that. Jude knew he was no hero. The truth was, apart from once – at Tattow's furious insistence – chopping firewood, and Ma had soon put a stop to that on the grounds that it was too dangerous, he'd hardly ever exerted himself physically before starting on this journey. He doubted he could kill one dragon, never mind two. Anyway, he had no weapons and balked at plunging his hands into the stew of corpses to obtain some.

There had to be another way.

He gauged the distance between himself and the tree. And dismissed making a run at it – leaping the ditch was one thing, but clambering over those scaly backs was quite another. Slip, fall against the tree and he'd be pulverised as the dragons struggled with each other. Failing that, one swipe with those powerful wings would, at the very least, break every bone in his body. With a shudder, he recalled the walls of the maze.

And then Jude wondered what would happen if the dragons were released.

He peered through the steamy mist as a fresh bout of noisy struggling ensued. Kid would call it a loony idea. It was certainly a terrifying one, and Jude was not short on fear. After all, release one dragon and it was likely to turn on him. On the other hand, it might rend its tormentor wing from limb, thus saving him the trouble of releasing the second. Or it might do something else he hadn't thought of.

Jude walked around the tree a considerable number of times chewing over the logic. Whatever happened, he couldn't stay here much longer: continually pinching his nostrils shut against the stench meant his body was running short of fresh air. When it came down to it, die this way or another, what did it really matter? As Kid said, it had always been a one way journey. She suddenly felt very close.

Jude took one step towards the dragons. And then another. He was nearest the head of the silver dragon, presently at rest, and he saw that its eyes were half open, watching him. They were proper lizard eyes, cold and expressionless, nothing like the round humanoid ones depicted on the door, but unlike any lizard he'd ever heard of, the dragon now began shedding copious tears.

"All right," Jude said, soothingly, extending one hand in the sure and certain knowledge that his whole arm wouldn't be an adequate meal for a hungry creature of this size. "Look, I'll try and set you free, but don't eat me alive, right?"

But already the dragons had regained enough strength for another bout of struggling. The whole cycle was repeated: they bucked and threshed, twisted and strained, and Jude hurriedly retreated as the air turned into mist and the stirred trench released even more noxious smells. When it was over he decided he might as well approach the red dragon with his proposal. The creature opened its eyes wide as Jude approached. It belched forth a few gentle puffs of steam and he was almost sure that it inclined its head in assent. Not that this meant a great deal – from the stories he'd heard, dragon promises weren't worth much.

He waited a while, thinking to make that leap onto the central platform immediately the next bout of activity was over, but this time the dragons lay still for so long that Jude finally understood they were keeping themselves in check, patiently waiting to see what he would do.

"Right," Jude told himself, feeling anything but. "Right, here we go then."

He slowly counted out twenty paces, hoping that would be enough of a distance in which to get up the momentum to clear the ditch.

There came a moment when Jude almost kept on walking but he turned in spite of his fear and began to run as fast he knew how, deliberately lengthening his stride, willing himself to clear the filthy ditch … He was in the air, almost flying … Yes! Yes! He was going to make it ... No. He landed just short of its far edge among the glooping squelching bodies, the flaccid limbs, the greenish livers, the ravelled guts and floating eyes. Squealing with horror he seized hold of something stout and grey immediately above his head and hauled himself out, only then realising that it was the white dragon's rear leg. The stuff was all over him. His stomach heaved. He couldn't bear to look down at himself. Neither could he bring himself to scrape it off. Instead he edged along the platform until he reached the white dragon's head. This close, its hide was thick and leathery; the nostrils were as big as his fist. The eye facing him watched unblinkingly as Jude examined the iron band. The tears continued to fall.

The ring was at least twice the size of Fareed's collar and seamless, there was no lock or fastening, and looked as if it had simply been pushed on to the creature's long snout, though who would have dared and why the dragon had let him, Jude couldn't imagine. Screwing up his courage, he tried to ease the thing off, but it was jammed behind some budding up-curved scales and wouldn't budge. Something was needed to hold the scales down as he pulled forward, then with any luck the ring should simply slip free. His fingers were too big. Jude glanced sideways and saw a solution: retching, almost vomiting, he reached down into the stew and brought out a length of broken rib. Even then it wasn't easy – the small scales were solid, he had to bear down with all his might to create space for the ring to come forward, and the ring itself was heavy. The dragon's scales began to gleam bright silver, almost fluid, as the ring finally moved down its snout. It slipped off, hung for a moment on the tip of the red dragon's tail, and then fell into the trench, throwing up a wall of putrefying matter.

The dragon reared up with a huge roar and let out an enormous blast of steam that almost toppled Jude back into the trench. It showed no aggression towards Jude, in fact it didn't acknowledge him at all. Taking this as a good sign, Jude scurried round and used the bone to ease off the red dragon's muzzle. It too was shedding tears and now its scales began to shine like liquid fire and it also reared up, beating its wings, when released. This time Jude had the foresight to put his back to the tree and cling to the lower branches.

And then both dragons did something he hadn't thought of: they dissolved.

Side by side they lumbered through the foul trench. Side by side they clambered out of it. Immediately, and without a backward glance, they were transformed into two raging torrents of water, one sparkling clear, the other faintly rust-coloured, that circled the tree seven times – sluicing the frightful contents of the ditch so that for a few moments the whole area was afloat with limbs and guts and skulls – and then swept into the cavern below with the great swoosh and gurgle of water too long dammed. Throughout the process Jude, who'd already been holding on to the tree for dear life, eyed the circling water, saw it was steadily rising, and desperately sought new finger holds in order to climb higher. Grabbing first one knotty branch and then another, he pulled himself almost to the top as the water reared up, tugging at his legs, swept past and was gone, leaving the ditch empty and the air fresh and clean. With only a little effort Jude was now able to reach out and pluck the wooden bowl from its lodging place and he cupped it in both hands, pleased by its homely familiarity and the memories it invoked. Tucking it inside his tunic he started to climb down, bent on finding a chalice fit for Ersay, but to Jude's dismay he discovered that the sheer force of the water had stripped the tree of every other vessel.

Back on solid ground he took out the bowl and examined it more closely, rubbing it on his tunic in the hope of making it more presentable. The cracks were far deeper than he remembered, the chips bigger, and long usage had worn away some of Da's carving. In addition, one side was badly scorched. It seemed a very poor thing to take back. And now it was too late. There would be no second chance. He couldn't replace it.

Jude lingered for a moment or two, watching as the ancient tree came back to life, its processes miraculously speeded up so that the flowers were already in full blow before he glumly climbed back down the root ladder into the scoured chamber below. He'd survived but it was no time for celebration: no splendid vessel and he still had to get back through the labyrinth. But some comfort came as he remembered that Blomweth had said the right vessel would speak to him of love, compassion and nurturing. As far as he was concerned, this shabby little bowl represented all of these things: Da's love for Ma that moved him to spend so many hours over its decoration; the nurturing and compassion shown by Ma and Bett when they tried to heal Osker with their various teas and potions; maybe even a little of all that when he himself had sent it with Osker on his final journey, for the dead man had next to nothing of his own to take. After Da died, there were only two things that gentled Ma's fierceness: one was her hand-fasting quilt, the other this bowl. It wasn't an ordinary bowl. That's why he'd so wanted to hold it again. And perhaps that was how such choices were made – that overwhelming conviction that this was the one he must hold and no other.

These thoughts heartened him and strengthened his resolve. He needed to get out of the labyrinth but it didn't seem right to retrace his steps. The great hall was not his goal, though he wasn't sure what was. Jude thought of Kid, and once more she seemed very close; close his eyes and he could almost imagine her calling his name. By looking carefully round the chamber, Jude found another passage entrance – almost opposite the one by which he'd entered – partially concealed by an interlaced network of roots. Clearly it hadn't been used in a long time. Yanking and cracking and snapping off the whippy growths, he worked a hole big enough to wriggle through.

A few steps in and the light changed to a curious muted red, which wasn't entirely pleasant. There were no bones here, but the width of this passage wasn't constant; the walls were warm and moist and squashy, they bulged and undulated in a way that suggested they were horribly alive. Soft fleshy folds hung from the roof. Brush against any surface and a tremor ran along the walls, making them close in and setting off a series of ripples that pushed him forward whether or not he wanted to go.

Jude was reminded him of a large caterpillar he'd once caught and which he kept for a while – watching fascinated as it moved up or down or across surfaces with a rhythm all of its own – before eating the thing and discovering its vile bitterness. But interest turned to fear as time went on, and Jude turned down this passage and then that, searching in vain for the way out. The movements of the walls became more pronounced, contracting dramatically, covering him with a viscous fluid even when he was careful not to touch them. They pushed into his shoulders, his arms, his legs. The roof sucked at his crown. The floor heaved and its peristaltic movements took him into blind alleys and down turnings he hadn't chosen. He dared not stop even for a moment, in case he was crushed or absorbed. And yet, all too soon, his exhaustion became such that he sank down in the middle of a passage, hunched over and gripping his knees. All fear finally left him. He'd done what he could: let the place do what it must, and quickly.

The whisperers returned.

Jude's grief turned it into a single voice, Kid's voice, calling his name. And it was his grief that made him answer.

"Kid! Kid! Where are you?"

"Jude?"

Jude knew that it was only his imagination playing tricks with him, but was happy to go along with it. Her voice was the one he chose to hear. It would probably be the last sound he ever heard, barring the persistent glooping as the walls exuded more fluid.

"Kid," he yelled, and again the voice answered, this time much fainter ... and then not at all. The illusion had faded. In spite of that Jude kept calling her name until his throat was sore and his voice grew hoarse. After that he sat in miserable silence and wept a little.

But soon it became clear that someone else was in the labyrinth. He made out muttering, sometimes fierce and sometimes plaintive, alternating with small noises of despair and disgust. Jude jumped to his feet. He'd gone past fear but he had not gone past hope. His heart beat slow and steady as the sounds grew louder and nearer.

A small dark silhouette emerged from a side passage, hunched over and whimpering softly. Confronted by Jude it hastily straightened and swaggered towards him.

"Hey, fat boy," said Kid. The hastily donned bravado conflicted with the tale told by her strained face and the dark hollows beneath her eyes.

"Kid?" He rubbed the tears and snot from his face. "Is that really you?"

"You ain't blubbing again?"

"Maybe a little," admitted Jude. "Didn't think I'd ever find a way out."

"I was always coming to get you, Jude. I told you so, right at the end."

And now Jude remembered the faint whisper in those moments of terrified frenzy before he tumbled into the abyss. He hadn't understood at the time, but then there'd been so much that didn't make sense …

"Thanks, Bug-head." He held open his arms and to his relief Kid allowed herself to be held. She allowed her hair to be stroked. She even permitted a gentle kiss. They stood in silence for a while. "How long you been looking for me?"

"Seems like forever and a day." Kid shrugged. "Don't matter. Didn't have nothing much else to do. You get Ersay's what's-it?"

"Is Ersay all right?" Jude took the little bowl from inside his tunic. The peculiar light emphasised all the flaws and none of the simple beauty so that it seemed even shabbier than before. A knot tightened in his stomach: to have come so far and then chosen the wrong vessel would be a terrible thing. He turned the bowl over in his hands, drawing what comfort he could from it.

"Don't look much," commented Kid. "Still, if that's what she wants. Yeh, Ersay's all right and back how she was. Him, too – though he ain't got a new eye or a new hand. No, nor a nicer way of carrying on, come to think of it. I done what needed doing, well, *we* did, and once you give her that bowl thing she'll put right all the damage what got done." After a moment she added: "You know we will forget all this when …"

"When?" he prompted.

"When it all gets as it will be. Perfect again. And that'll be thanks to us."

"Oh," said Jude. "Will it?" He guessed the time for caring about being called stupid was long past. "Me, I just kept going. There never seemed any choice once we'd started – but I never really understood why we had to do any of it."

"Should have asked," Kid said, smugly. "Ersay says …"

Jude bit back a tart comment. "Let's get out of here."

Kid laughed in his face. "Just remember," she said, "that for a short time you were Lord of the Heavens and I was Queen of the Earth."

"Oh," muttered Jude. "I see." But he didn't. And he was no longer sure that it mattered. Everything had been done to the best of his ability; understanding why wouldn't necessarily have helped.

Kid stirred impatiently. "Follow me," she said, turning around. "I can find the way out." Clutching his wrist, she strode confidently back the way she'd come. After a few paces, she looked over her shoulder and there was laughter in her voice as she called: "Don't look back, fat boy. Whatever you do, don't look back."

Now Jude saw that Kid was following a trail, not of silver this time, but something much more homely. Bett had emphasised that a clew was needed, a thread to guide the hero out of the labyrinth. She'd spoken of spider silk, but Kid's seemed to be made out of knotted rags, faded flowers and patched geometrics, and before long he recognised it as the last fragments of Ma's old hand-fasting quilt ripped into thin strips and knotted into a long pale marker that lay along the floor and twisted round corners, left, right, right again, through myriad twists and turns that Jude was sure he'd never have successfully navigated alone.

They moved quickly until the passage abruptly narrowed, the roof bore down upon them and the floor rose up to meet it.

"Quick," said Kid, and pulled her hand away. "Down on your knees. Crawl."

The walls rippled and pushed them on. Moments later, they passed, heads first, from the darkness into a warm soft night, the sky alight with stars.

# 10

More darkness, Jude thought morosely, keeping a tight hold on the bowl, but at least this time he wasn't alone. Besides, he quickly realised, this was a different type of darkness altogether with none of the brooding menace of those passages leading in and out of the labyrinth. This was the dark before the dawn, soul flight time, that fleeting period where a curiously intense absence of light marks the changeover between the dominion of the moon and that of the sun.

A tiny breeze played over his skin. It was not cold, simply refreshing, but it was enough to make him realise that every last stitch of his clothes had gone. The state they'd been in this was no great loss, though where he'd get more Jude couldn't imagine. He wondered if it was just him lying here stripped to the skin: he didn't enjoy being at a disadvantage where Kid was concerned. Cautiously reaching an arm in her direction, Jude encountered bare midriff.

"Here, what's your bluddy game?" she demanded, shoving his hand away.

"We're naked," he whispered.

"Yeh, think I hadn't noticed? So what? Apart from all that fat, you ain't got nothing I ain't seen before."

Jude bit his tongue and wished for more light – and soon.

"Anyway," said Kid, after a short silence, "why you whispering?"

"No reason." Jude grinned into the darkness. Moments later, his gaze slid sideways as the glint of daylight appeared on the horizon, diluting the darkness enough for him to make out Kid's lithe form curled next to him.

"I ain't blind," announced Kid. "Find something else to stare at."

Jude grinned again. He could wait. Sitting up, he watched the sky slowly lighten, ushering in a gold and apricot sunrise streaked with rosy pinks and soft trails of pale violet. Tyrod stood silhouetted black as pitch and gigantic against the intense brightness with his coat held open just as on that first morning by the river. And now Jude saw that they were back on the hill. The tower had gone, not a trace of it remained, but there was far more hilltop than when he and Kid had desperately dragged all that was left of the wagon right to the tower's doorway with the land being rapidly devoured behind them.

Tyrod's enormous shadow grew broader and taller as the sun climbed up the sky stretching, shadow arms flung wide, right across the hilltop until it reached to where they were sitting and beyond. Kid rolled away into a patch of sunlight. Jude stood up and looked around. There was land in every direction, and as far as he could see it was entirely free of holes, rifts and chasms. And yet, it wasn't right: in spite of the bright early morning light the whole countryside was bathed in gloomy twilight shades of grey and black, dead and chilly as last night's fire ash. Even worse, though it was hard to be sure, he couldn't make out a single living thing, plant or animal.

"This doesn't look much like perfect to me," he grumbled.

Kid raised her head. "That's what the bowl-thing's for, stupid. Why d'you think she sent you to get it?"

Jude didn't answer. Shielding his eyes against the intense light, he purported to be scanning the cold grey landscape whilst actually examining Kid's nakedness through half closed eyes.

"Bluddy stop that."

"What?" Jude attempted to look bewildered.

"This." Kid sat up and stared unblinkingly at him.

"Lay off. When was I doing that?"

Kid continued to stare. After a time this proved so disturbing that Jude lay down and stared at the sky, which was clear blue and completely cloudless. It was odd having nothing to do and nowhere to go.

And then Ersay stood over him taller and even more beautiful than he remembered, dressed all in white. Jude jumped to his feet and bowed his head, momentarily embarrassed by his nakedness.

"So," said Ersay, and Jude looked up and forgot everything else as he looked into her eyes, "my unlikely champion has completed his task and returned from the Otherworld. That is a rare thing indeed. Many have tried and failed." She smiled directly into his face and Jude thought he might melt from the joy of it. "What have you brought me, Jude?"

All Jude's previous misgivings rushed back. If only he'd brought one of the golden chalices. "I'm sorry …" he shamefacedly proffered the bowl.

"Why do you apologise?" Ersay looked at the little bowl carefully, turning it round in her hands to examine the wreath of oak-corn, running her fingers along the grain of the wood, holding it to her cheek as though to absorb its essence. "This is indeed a vessel beyond price and well chosen: made with love, given with love, used with compassion and sacrificed out of friendship."

Tyrod came back to stand beside her, fastening his coat shut. "You did well, whelp, to emerge victorious where so many seasoned warriors have failed. Even I, ruler of the skies, summoner of souls and the bringer of victory, the one who knows all things past, present, and yet to come, was not sure you would prevail."

Jude looked at him sidelong, wondering if this was supposed to be some sort of joke – even he could see that Tyrod had contradicted his own omniscience – but the huge man's stern profile made him think otherwise. Kid nudged him and Jude hastily muttered his thanks. Then he opened his mouth to deliver a speech he'd been mentally rehearsing on and off since his sojourn in the bone labyrinth concerning Tyrod's damning accusations. A look from Tyrod silenced him.

"I know your thoughts, boy. Listen well. There was no fear until man's greed got the better of him. Remember no one can own any part of the earth – to think they can is an outrageous presumption, for ownership by one means loss of natural birthright by countless others. That is the first rule. The second is: take what you need and no more. Enough was provided for all. Enough is about to be provided again, more than enough." Tyrod nodded towards Ersay, who stood looking out over the blighted land. "It remains to be seen whether what little is left of your race has learned the lesson. This may be your last chance. Even she will eventually run out of patience."

"But we never wanted to own …" began Jude, who had learned the first rule at Ma's knee, before remembering how regularly and deliberately the second had been flouted.

"Exactly," said Tyrod. "Now be silent and watch."

Turning towards the north, Ersay cupped the bowl in both hands and raised it to her lips. She blew into it, a long, steady outbreath – that Jude was almost sure he could see filling the bowl and pulsing out onto the land – turning slowly to face each of the cardinal points.

"Now she will heal the earth," said Kid at his elbow, her soft hair brushing against him. Jude looked at her and almost missed the moment when the earth came alive again, but then he felt grass beneath his feet and saw the entire landscape change from grey to a thousand shades of green as plants and herbs covered its barrenness, swiftly followed by bushes and trees. There were flowers, too, so that the green was dappled with burst of colours bright as stars. But there were no houses, not even the hint of a ruin, no tracks or highways, no fences and no walls.

When she had finished, Ersay rested awhile before she blew again. This time all the small creatures that had taken refuge in the wagon streamed away from the hilltop, two by two. First the insects, butterflies, dragonflies, ladybirds, and all the myriad bugs and beetles Jude had no names for, and then the birds. Most circled and flapped away to fill the valleys with their songs and squawks, but the two white doves stayed and began rootling among the grass stalks at Ersay's feet.

"Birds?" muttered Jude, aghast. "What's perfect about them?"

Tyrod glared. "The birds are harmless. They only gave back what man had foisted upon them." He stood before Ersay and bowed his head and she blew across the bowl's rim until his huge black ravens appeared in mid-air and dropped on to his shoulders.

Ersay blew again and animals appeared at a distance, playing or grazing on the slopes of the hill, burrowing into the earth, making for the shelter of the trees, and a sprightly horse that might have been Fareed – Jude hoped so – galloped with its mate across a forest clearing.

Now the landscape was ablaze with every colour imaginable. Lakes and ponds and rivers reflected the cloudless blue of the sky. In the woods and forests the trees shone with the bright sap green of early summer. How Ma would have loved this beautiful new world. Jude wondered what she would have done to it. He wondered what he would do.

"There," said Ersay, and her dress reflected the many greens and was strewn with all the flowers of awakening spring: aconites, snowdrops, the regal purples and gold of crocuses, daffodils. It shimmered and clung as she set down the bowl.

"You can see how well you chose, Jude. This was indeed the right vessel. Now, I will return your gift."

She produced the apple Jude had given her on the day he'd balked at kissing the ancient hag Ersay had become. He blushed to remember it. In retrospect, that had been the last day of an over-long childhood.

Ersay rolled the apple along the grass and where it stopped, a tree sprang up. It looked exactly like the tree at the heart of the labyrinth – far too old to be so very young. And like that tree it budded, flowered and bore fruit at once: beautiful apples like the ones in the orchard by the river.

"That's a seal of my promise to you," said Ersay. "You will have all you need to sustain you. Go forward in peace and stay in peace."

"It is all perfect," said Kid, "perfect and new, just as you said it would be."

"Yes." Ersay looked at her and a flicker of sadness crossed the beautiful face. "And yet, you have brought with you something of the old world, Kid."

Kid shook her head. "No." She spread her arms, demonstrating her nakedness to underline the impossibility of Ersay's statement.

"You carry within you a new life child conceived in terror and sorrow."

Jude watched, horrified, as Kid looked down at herself, looked up again with wide eyes brimming with tears. Anger began to build in him. He clenched his fists and ground his teeth.

"Something is always carried over." Ersay sighed. "Let us hope that this child does not bring with it the seeds of the earth's destruction."

"If so, then it will be as it has always been," said Tyrod, resigned. The ravens jigged and danced on his shoulders,

"I will kill it," blurted out Jude, glowing with rage as he thought of No-ears and Dappled-skin and all the others, and what they had done to Kid. "We want no part of them here."

Kid shook her head. "No, Jude."

"The choice is yours," said Ersay, "as always. But remember every child is born in innocence. It plays no part in any sin of conception. Besides, such an act of destruction would not bode well for the future of your new world."

"I will teach him well," said Kid. She put her hand on her stomach.

"Her," said Ersay.

"I will watch over her," added Kid. "She need never learn hate or cruelty."

"And I will try to be a father to her," said Jude, doubtfully, thinking he did not know how and trying his hardest to remember how it was with Da. Tyrod thumped him between the shoulders, sending him staggering.

"Boy, you have taken my part in the sacred marriage between heaven and earth, you have ventured alone into the underworld, you have conquered the death and life labyrinth – do you not think you are capable of teaching a squealing brat how to live in the world?"

"Dunno," said Jude.

"We'll manage," said Kid. "There will be no one against us, no one to chase us or imprison us, no one to make us run and hide in fear of our lives."

"That's right," agreed Ersay. "Remember also, both of you, that neither one is set above the other. Always remember that you rescued each other in your different hours of need."

"Yeh," said Kid, but she looked sidelong at Jude and the look was doubtful.

"Yes," said Jude, with conviction, remembering that he'd once laughed at the idea of Kid rescuing him. "I won't forget. Is there anything else you want me to do?"

"One last thing," said Ersay. "Jude, you always loved fireside stories. Weave all these things into a tale that will live on in the hearts of those that come after you. But never forget that a tale can't be held prisoner. Once told, it belongs to the world and can be shaped to fit different purposes. It can be a lesson, but also a weapon and a curse." She laid her hands on their shoulders. "Now, Kid and Jude, we must bid you farewell."

"You're not leaving us?" Jude's eyes opened wide. The old fears returned. It was a new world. Anything could happen. How would they manage?

"'Course she is," said Kid. "Just you and me now, fat boy." Her chin went up. "We'll be all right."

"No!" Jude jettisoned all pride. "Please don't go," he begged. "Stay with us. Don't leave us here all alone. Not so soon."

Tyrod sighed, growled something deep in his throat and glared at Jude. "You shame yourself."

Ersay frowned. "Will the earth not still be beneath your feet, Jude? Will its beauty not surround you? Will it not provide everything you need to sustain life?"

Jude hung his head. "Suppose so."

She came closer. "And can you not feel its heartbeat within you, pulsing in time with your own?"

"Maybe." Jude wasn't sure.

"Wait," cried Kid. "Are there others like us?"

Ersay nodded. "Far flung and few. They hope to find you as much as you want to find them."

"It may take a while," said Tyrod, with a sardonic grin. "Now, I need to cut myself a stout staff." He took a few steps, clearly impatient to be gone.

"How will we know where to …?"

Tyrod laughed and produced Bett's bag of runes. "Use these. Told you I'd return them to you by-and-by. The answers to most questions can be determined by use of the rune stones. The others, your heart should hold the answers to. Catch!"

Jude reached up to catch the bag, but it slipped through his fingers spilling the stones on to the grass. He stooped quickly to gather them up and Kid dropped to her knees to help him. When he straightened, both Ersay and Tyrod had gone. All the creatures had left, too, every last one. They were alone.

"We'll be all right," repeated Kid, laying her hand on his arm. "Come on, fat boy, no blubbing."

"Yeh," said Jude, doubtfully. Reaching up, he picked two perfectly matched apples from the tree and passed one to Kid. They both chewed thoughtfully for a while and gradually Jude's fear of the unknown lost its edge. Kid was right: already his memories of what had gone before were losing shape, fading. "Yeh, we'll be fine."

He took a deep breath. "Right, Bug-head, what shall we do next?"

***THE END***

## *Also by Liza Granville:*

### *Until the Skies Fall*

Laz is a young man in a post-apocalyptic England where the disastrous results of genetic engineering are evident everywhere. He is persuaded his destiny is to save the world from a threatening Death Star. Along with his companions he sets out on an epic and perilous journey. They encounter strange remnants of previous societies; each one convinced it represents the only true and proper form of humanity. Can Laz and his friends survive the dangers en route and the hostility of those they meet? Can Laz reach his destination before it is too late?

Until the Skies Fall is a thought provoking and intriguing tale narrated with humour and great compassion. It is a truly different view and account of a very possible future that questions what it is to be human.

paperback ISBN:: 978-1-906609-00-9
ebook ISBN: 978-1-906609-01-6

## *Also by Liza Granville:*

### *The House in the Riddle*

Sorrel and Mark, her controlling, apocalypse-obsessed husband, arrived at the ruined barn and cottage chosen by him to be their final refuge in the coming End of Days only to discover that the property has its own secrets.

Can Sorrel use these to break free of her past and find a life for herself? In this novel the lives of the mismatched pair intersect with those of several equally odd characters as their drama is played out.

A well-written psychological thriller gripping to the last page.

paperback ISBN: 978-1-906609-14-6
ebook ISBN: 978-1-906609-15-3

Lightning Source UK Ltd.
Milton Keynes UK
12 June 2010

155498UK00001B/14/P